INNOCENT DEAD

A DR HARRISON LANE MYSTERY
BOOK 4

GWYN BENNETT

Storm
PUBLISHING

ALSO BY GWYN BENNETT

The Dr Harrison Lane Mysteries

1. *Broken Angels*

2. *Beautiful Remains*

3. *Deadly Secrets*

4. *Innocent Dead*

5. *Perfect Beauties*

6. *Captive Heart*

7. *Winter Graves*

8. *Dark Whispers*

The DI Clare Falle Series

1. *Lonely Hearts*

2. *Home Help*

3. *Death Bond*

The Villagers

1

———

The sound of the drum filled everything.

Ba bam ba ba bam.

Her heart was beating so fast, it hurt.

Ba bam ba ba bam, ba bam ba ba bam, ba bam ba ba bam...

His hands beat down on the animal skin drum. Fast. Rhythmic.

Ba bam ba ba bam, ba bam ba ba bam, ba bam ba ba bam...

Sweat ran down his black skin.

The juju priest stood before them welcoming the spirits. Face tipped towards the ceiling. Eyes white. Behind him, the offerings of money and food lay in front of the altar, where small black wooden sculptures of the spirit gods, clothed in skins, stared into the room.

Terror rose in her stomach, into her chest, threatening to choke her throat. She needed to hide her fear.

Memories of her oath ceremony back home with the juju priest in Edo, Nigeria, came back to her. She'd given him hair and fingernails, as well as blood, and in return he'd kept a part of her soul and given her luck and the promise of a better life in Europe. The other women in the room with her had all gone through the same oath ritual. Tonight, they were being reminded of their promise and its price.

The juju priest's chest convulsed with deep breaths, his body heaving and his dreadlocks swinging back and forth.

The drum seemed to beat faster still.

Ba bam ba ba bam, ba bam ba ba bam, ba bam ba ba bam...

The drum stopped, and he closed his eyes, raising his arms aloft.

In the silence, it appeared her own heart had taken on the beat of the drum. It thumped so hard in her chest that she was sure he would hear it.

Suddenly, the priest dropped his arms and his eyelids shot open. They were no longer the eyes of a mere human.

The juju priest began his prayer.

He rose from the floor and approached the women, who knelt before him in a semi-circle, not daring to look in his eyes.

He stood in front of each of them, one by one, and called on the spirits, blowing onto the plate of white powder in his hands. The powder flew into the face of each woman, marking her. Showing the spirits whose soul he was asking them to keep watch over.

She could never make the mistake again. Her soul, her family's safety back home, were all at risk. The juju priest had shown his power. The white lady, the one who had said she would help her, she was dead. He'd cursed her and a week later claimed her soul.

Nobody could help her. No one was safe. She had made her oath, and she had to keep it.

2

Even by Dr Harrison Lane's standards, the setting was atmospheric for an occult ritual. The small semi-ruined gothic chapel was clothed in ivy, its thin tendrils grasping firmly onto anything in their path with supernatural strength. Two grotesque creatures, mouths open, flanked the doorway. The horned stone beasts, pain etched across their grey features, stared down at all who walked beneath as ivy spewed from their mouths.

Harrison stood at the start of the short, overgrown path which led to the chapel's doorway. He was flanked by the tall, but slender frame of Mr Roger Thurlow, headmaster of the private school in whose grounds they both stood. In Harrison's experience, school head teachers were calm, serene creatures who, used to dealing with hundreds of adolescent individuals with minds of their own, rarely showed stress. Mr Thurlow appeared not to be one of those men, or perhaps the situation had brought on a major, uncharacteristic episode.

The headmaster spoke, dark circles clouding his eyes. 'I

need to know what we're dealing with here, Dr Lane. The reputation of this school could be severely damaged if we discover a satanic cult has been operating among the students.'

Harrison fully understood his concern. The telephone call he'd received earlier that morning had told of sacrifices and occult rituals. Dangerous enough when adults were involved, let alone a school full of pre-pubescent boys.

*　*　*

ROGER THURLOW LOOKED at the large, muscular man next to him and wrung his hands together. His leather-clad saviour had arrived just ten minutes before on a black Harley Davidson bike that had caused students' eyes to be distracted, books to be set aside, and teachers' eyebrows to be raised at windows. Even the police car that had pulled up at the entrance that morning had been more discreet than the big throbbing motorbike. He had to keep this under wraps; he also had to find out what had been happening in his school.

Dr Harrison Lane, head of the Metropolitan Police's Ritualistic Behavioural Crime unit, was not what he'd expected. Roger found this was often the case nowadays. Individuality was having a renaissance. It wasn't like things had been in the 70s and 80s, when everyone had to conform to be taken seriously, or even be accepted in society. He'd noticed it in his students; the homogenous product they'd once pumped out at the end of every school year had started to sprout quirks and characteristics which made for a far more diverse range of individuals. Wasn't it Shakespeare who said, *To thine own self be true?*

He wondered what direction his own personality might have taken if he'd been given more freedom to express himself. As for Dr Lane, his job wouldn't have existed even a few years ago, and he doubted the police would have even considered allowing this renegade into their fold. He could just see a small brown eagle inked on the back of Dr Lane's neck. His own brother-in-law had spent thirty-five years in the Met, and if he wasn't mistaken, neck tattoos were still frowned on. Still, Harrison came well recommended. The headmaster hoped he wouldn't disappoint.

'Who has been up the path and inside?' Dr Lane turned to him and Roger found himself fixed by an intelligent stare, which did nothing to help his nerves.

'Myself, of course, and our groundskeeper who alerted me, plus the police officer who came this morning. He said he'd worked with you on a case before and that you would know exactly what's gone on. There were all those rumours a few years ago about satanic cults in north London. I don't want this getting into the papers.'

Dr Lane had returned his gaze forward, and the headmaster found himself peering expectantly at the man's profile for some kind of reassurance. His jawline was firm, sculptured.

'You wait here,' was all he got in response.

* * *

HARRISON STEPPED AWAY from the distracting intensity of the headmaster by his side and breathed in deeply. He needed to concentrate and put Roger Thurlow's nervous anxiety out of his mind. The path would be difficult to read, but not impossible with his tracking skills.

He centred his mind and focused. His shoulders involuntarily rotating to ease the tension that had built as he'd negotiated his way through London's traffic. Breathing deeply again, he filled his lungs with the aroma of damp autumnal vegetation. It was almost winter, and the air had a bite to it, slicing into his chest with a refreshing burn.

Harrison dropped his eyes to the ground. He'd already looked at the headmaster's feet, and he knew the style of shoes that a uniformed police officer wore, so he surmised that the rugged boot prints which led down the middle of the path had been left there by the groundsman.

Slowly, he walked forward, studying the patterns of the footprints in the mud. His eyes stayed focused on the path, only occasionally rising to look at the bushes and plants that were vying to suffocate any free space around them. Dried grasses and thistles, brambles, and nettles. Harrison stopped to inspect an area of vegetation where the last remnants of that season's blackberries were rotting amid the thorns.

Onwards.

Just inside the entrance to the chapel, he saw a large white candle lying abandoned in the dust and debris.

The chapel itself smelled of the damp vegetation which clung to its stone skeleton. Rotting wood, which had presumably fallen from the roof where a large hole now let in the daylight and elements, was strewn on the floor and leaning against the walls.

Harrison stopped again, taking the time to examine the whole scene in front of him. A circle with a pentagram was drawn into the dust and debris on the floor, small tea light candles forming its ring and a ouija board at its centre. A simple stone altar was illuminated by a ray of daylight coming through the hole in the roof. This chapel had never been luxurious in its construction and decor. It could have only accommodated around ten to a dozen people at most. Possibly the teaching staff, or perhaps the school had once been run by monks.

What had apparently alarmed the headmaster most, besides the ouija board and ritualistic circle, was the sacrifice which lay across the altar, and the large knife lying in the dust in front of it.

Harrison always steeled himself when he investigated satanic rituals like this. Sacrifices took many forms, animal or human, and involved a detachment from modern societal values which spoke to powerful ancient beliefs. He'd seen some terrible and sad scenes in his career, but there was one ritualistic sacrifice which never left him. The one he'd witnessed when he was just a child.

He pushed away the knot that tried to form in his gut at that thought. Today would be easier. One small blessing this time was that it couldn't be human, otherwise the officer this morning would have called in the Serious Crime squad and the area would be crawling with forensics.

Harrison sniffed at the air, trying to distinguish the unusual from the natural environment. A sweet scent drifted towards him on the breeze from the hole in the roof.

Slowly, he stepped towards the altar, where another abandoned candle lay next to the knife. He could see the sacrifice properly now. A dead bird. Harrison dropped to a crouch to get a closer look. It was a male pheasant with rich chestnut-gold feathers on its breast and the blue-green petrol of its head accented by red eye patches.

Harrison's concentration dropped, a rare occurrence when he was viewing a crime scene, and an even rarer smile crept onto his lips. He reached for the candle and brought it to his nose. The smile crept higher.

Dr Lane turned back to the circle and pentagram, looking in more detail at the scuffs and footprints in the dirt. He stopped to investigate a small piece of charred white paper, picking it up and bringing it to his nose, before dropping it back down onto the floor.

When he was finished, he stepped out of the chapel holding the candle he'd picked up at the altar, and walked towards the headmaster.

'Have you heard of pomegranate noir?' He asked the headmaster, who looked like he had stopped breathing while he waited for Harrison's report.

'No. I don't think so. Is it a satanic ritual?'

'No. It's a Jo Malone scent, used in candles just like this one. You've nothing to worry about here, Mr Thurlow.'

'What? I don't understand.'

The headmaster reached out for the candle Harrison proffered and sniffed it.

'It's a nice scent,' Harrison said to him. 'Expensive candles. I think one of your parents will be missing a couple from their home, along with some other items. This was just a first-time attempt at an occult ritual by a group of your students, who are almost certainly regretting the idea this morning.'

'How can you tell?'

'The candles are not satanic, as I've explained. The knife used isn't a ritual knife or athame; it's a kitchen knife. As for our sacrifice, I think there was a major flaw in the students' plan. The idea of a sacrifice is to spill blood, often to drink it, but also to offer the spirit of an animal or human at the point of death to whatever demon or god you are attempting to worship. The pheasant in there had been shot and hung days ago. There was no fresh blood to spill.'

'Thank goodness,' Roger Thurlow breathed. 'So, nothing endemic in the school.'

'You need to look for a group of four students. It's likely they listen to heavy metal music. One of them has white wax on their trainer, and one has an orange woollen jumper. I suspect all four might have trouble getting to sleep tonight.'

'How do you know all this?' the headmaster asked, wide-eyed. There wasn't scepticism in his voice, more amazement.

'You looked, but you didn't see.'

Harrison beckoned him to follow. 'In here, I can see four areas in the dirt on the floor where someone has sat. At some point, they were all spooked.'

Harrison walked over to near the altar and pointed at some scuffing in the dust that interrupted a trail of white wax.

'One boy had got up and had hold of the candle which you now have. Something made him jump or caused him to tip the candle, allowing the wax to pour out. You can see the deep well which would have held the molten wax. It went across his shoe, as you can see from the trainer print, which interrupts the trail of wax.

'From here, he ran straight out. I can see the panic in his footprints – he was skidding around here. There are signs the other three also got up in a hurry, and I suspect that's when the other candle was knocked over.'

The headmaster looked to where Harrison was pointing, his face quizzical as he strained to see what Harrison was showing him. 'The orange jumper?' he queried.

'The path is overgrown with brambles down one side. In their haste to leave, one of them snagged their jumper. I found a strand of the wool caught on the bush and it's recent, so I'd be pretty sure it was one of our apprentice satanists. There are also areas along the path where vegetation has been flattened in the direction they would have taken leaving the chapel. They ran, probably slipping and bumping into each other to get away as fast as they could.'

'Amazing,' Roger exclaimed, impressed. 'How about the heavy metal music, then?'

'It's part of the scene. A lot of youngsters who are into their heavy metal try it out to some degree. That's the one thing I don't have evidence of, but it's an educated guess.'

'This is such a relief, thank you. I can talk to my house staff; between us we'll identify them.'

'There is one more thing,' Harrison added, 'I think they were smoking marijuana. There's evidence of a spliff in here. I'm presuming that's from our satanic foursome and the chapel isn't a secret smoking den. Worth keeping an eye on.'

IT MAY NOT HAVE BEEN all good news, but with the evidence bundled together and the case solved, Harrison left the decidedly relieved headmaster to hunt down the four students. As Harrison rode out of the school and headed to his office, he wished that all his cases were as easy as this one.

3

Harrison had given Ryan the day off. His assistant would far rather be helping him out in the unit, but their contract with the London Met Police was drawing to a close and Ryan's reluctance to take a holiday had resulted in him accruing several weeks' leave. Soon they would be starting their Ritualistic Behavioural Crime unit over at the National Crime Agency, and he didn't want Ryan missing out on what was owed him.

As it was, Ryan had only agreed to taking two days off so he could sort out his flat. He was moving closer to their new base and if his desk was anything to go by, his flat would be full of food, snacks, and tech equipment, with his bins overflowing.

Harrison was going to help him move his stuff out in a few weeks. He'd already booked the van and gone with Ryan to his new place. He'd also suggested that they walked the route to the new office together, and Ryan had gratefully accepted. They never talked about his agoraphobia specifically. It was their unspoken understanding, and Harrison knew when to offer support and when to let Ryan just get on with it. This was going to be a big upheaval for him. For them both.

He flicked on the light switch, illuminating his office in the basement of New Scotland Yard. As his shelves of books and ritualistic relics appeared from the darkness, it reminded Harrison he was also going to need to shift all this out. He'd have to store it in his flat. He knew that most people struggled when they came face-to-face with voodoo dolls, skulls, and ouija boards, even if he explained it had been con artists and criminals who had used them. He wanted his new colleagues to be working with them, not avoiding them. The troubles they'd had with cleaners over the years, refusing to even enter the room, had reminded him how you never knew what kind of beliefs and fears motivated people.

Some books would need to come with him; the reference manuals on witchcraft, satanic rites, and shamans. His religious symbolism research was essential on a day-to-day basis. It was the decorative memorabilia he could live without, and which would need to be packed up and stored, for now.

This morning's visit to the school had given him some light relief after the last couple of weeks. It hadn't been so much his caseload, as revelations from his own past that had rocked his usually solid state of mind. Most importantly, he knew the journey of discovery was a long way from being over. There was an express train of revelations heading his way, which could derail him completely. He still wasn't sure how or even if he could stop it.

His first reaction had been to hide and hope It all steamed on past, but he knew that wasn't an option. It wasn't that he was afraid. If anything, he welcomed it. A lifetime of not remembering or understanding elements of your own past was draining. He resented that it took up head space. The difficulty was to come up with a plan to stop a train when you had no clear idea of which track it was running on and which station it would end up at. He wasn't someone who asked for help often, but he knew he might need it this time – and that involved knowing who to trust.

Harrison filled the kettle at the little sink in the corner of his office. He opened up his Pukka tea box, a gift from Detective Chief Inspector Sandra Barker. Yesterday, she'd emailed him a few smiling photos of her and her daughter, Gemma, up in Durham. He recognised the backdrop of the cathedral and Palace Green from his time there just a week or so ago. They looked like they'd had a good weekend together and she'd reported back that Gemma seemed to have now settled into university life. Sandra had sent him the tea as a thank you for helping ease that process, and for assisting Durham police with their phantom monk murder enquiry. Harrison knew Gemma would be fine. She'd just wanted her mother to spend some time with her.

He liked his gift. He wasn't exactly easy to buy for, but Sandra knew him well. They'd worked on enough cases together. His eyes ranged over the various flavours of herbal tea on offer and he settled for a Tulsi Clarity. The mix of tulsi herbs, also known as holy basil, seemed appropriate after this morning, and he enjoyed their flavour.

He had just sat at his desk, letting out a sigh of satisfaction at the tranquillity of his office space, when it was decimated by the door being flung open and the blond-headed vision of Detective Sergeant Jack Salter bursting through it.

'We need a word,' he said to Harrison, closing the door quickly behind himself. His expression was serious – definitely not the Jack that Harrison was used to. He was smartly dressed as always, hair brushed, shirt ironed, but there was concern on his face. Jack glanced over to check if Ryan was in residence and then grabbed the spare chair and sat down.

'Morning, Jack,' Harrison replied, raising an eyebrow. He leant back in his chair and studied his colleague and friend, wondering what was coming next.

'I need you to be honest with me, Harrison. I won't be able to help you if you're not.'

'Fine,' Harrison replied.

'I mean it. You've got to be on the level. We can still sort this if you are.'

Harrison felt a niggle of concern. Had the DNA results come through on the items they'd found in Freda Manning's safe deposit box? He wouldn't have been surprised if Jack thought he was doing Harrison a favour and got them rushed through the system. Freda, one half of the evil pair who he was convinced had murdered his mother, was dying of cancer, but he knew she would still try to destroy him if she could. It wasn't enough that she'd nearly ruined his life already once before. She wanted to make sure she did the job properly this time.

After Jack and Harrison had visited her in the hospice, she'd sent the key for the box directly to Jack. Inside was a bloodied knife, a necklace, and a torn piece off a white dress.

A flashback to the moment he'd remembered at Nunhead Cemetery filled his mind. Harrison, just seven years old, standing over the body of Annette Ward, who had been part of Desmond and Freda Mannings' cult along with Harrison and his mother. Her lifeless eyes staring at him as she lay across the stone in her white dress, sacrificed as part of the sick satanic ritual presided over by the Mannings. His mother's face, watching wide-eyed and terrified, still haunted him. Shortly after, they'd escaped to America, just Harrison and his mother, building a new life with his stepfather Joe. Yet for some reason that he still didn't understand, they'd returned to the UK where she too would be murdered.

Only, Harrison was no longer sure it was the Mannings who'd plunged the knife into Annette. In his memory, it was his own hands which held the knife. A detail no one else knew – not Jack and not even Harrison until recently.

Jack had been helping Harrison to catch his mother's killers, but Harrison felt the growing dread that it would be him who ended up in a trap. That the Mannings had kept the evidence because it linked him to Annette's murder.

'They're looking for her, Harrison. She's a sick woman and needs to be in the hospice. Tell me you haven't done anything stupid? Is she still alive?' Jack pulled him back to the here and now.

'What are you talking about?' Harrison asked.

'Look, I'd feel the same way. If I thought someone had murdered my mother and I could get to her after years of searching, then I'd probably want to make her suffer too, but you know it's not right. It could end your career, for one thing.'

Harrison sighed. 'I've no idea what you're talking about.'

'Freda Manning is missing from the hospice. You were the last person to visit her and now she's gone. Where is she?'

The words hung between them for a moment as Harrison processed what Jack had just said. His friend studied Harrison's face.

'I honestly don't know. I left her in her room.'

'Seriously? You're telling me you went all the way up to Harrogate again just for another quick chat?'

'How long has she been missing for? It must be Desmond.

He must have come for her. I knew he wouldn't just leave her there.'

'Nobody saw Desmond. You were the last person to visit, and she couldn't just walk out. She's too sick.'

'I'm telling you, Jack, it's nothing to do with me.'

'OK, then why did you go back? You saw her last week. The woman is poison to you and yet you went back again. Why?'

'I had my reasons.'

Jack smacked his forehead with his palm and glared across the desk at his friend. His face was growing red with frustration. Harrison had never seen him like this and he was concerned that he seemed to be the cause of it. The usually active laughter lines around Jack's eyes and mouth sat impotent and in their place was a frown.

'I don't get it. I'm trying to help you here.' Jack said to him.

'I know. Thank you, but I'm telling you, I left Freda in her room.'

'The police up there are investigating. Someone must have carried her or put her in a wheelchair. They're probably going to want to speak to you because unless there are any other indications, she didn't leave voluntarily.'

'Fair enough.'

Harrison went quiet, thinking back on his visit. Picturing the wizened old woman in the bed. Jack was right. She wasn't capable of leaving that room on her own. Had he missed something? Or someone?

'That it?' Jack goaded him now.

'I think we'll find out soon enough what's going on. They'd have planned this. We'll hear from Freda or Desmond again.'

Jack shook his head at him and sighed, collapsing back into his chair. Fight gone. Resigned.

'Well, in the meantime, you're needed. There's been a serious assault on a Black South African man. He's over here on a visa for six months and the initial investigation found two white men specifically targeted him because they believe he put a curse on their church and murdered a woman. It's all a bit messy. He's in a coma in hospital.

'The two men are claiming it was self-defence. They've been charged with racially motivated assault, and are just awaiting their first court appearance. Allegedly, they witnessed him putting the curse on the dead woman. The initial investigation was looking at it from the racial motivation, but they've since found what looks like some kind of voodoo paraphernalia at his flat, and some of the other people who go to the church are also falling ill. It's causing a minor panic in that community, which could blow up into a big problem if we don't get to the bottom of what's going on. What we don't want are reprisal attacks and riots.

'We're investigating both the potential murder and the serious assault. We need you to take a look at what this guy's been doing over here. If he's up to no good, we need to see who else is involved. Are there other victims, and if the dead woman is even connected at all?'

'Voodoo? What people nowadays mean as voodoo isn't generally South African, it has its roots in west Africa and places like Haiti, Jamaica, Dominican Republic, or New Orleans, but it's been sensationalised. There's a lot of hype and misconception which breeds ignorance, especially culturally. But there are other similar religions it could be.'

'That's why we need you to take a look,' Jack replied. 'We have no idea what we're dealing with right now. The big fear is we could have another boy Adam in the Thames case,' he added; referring to the torso of a young African boy found several years before and linked to child trafficking and ritualistic murders.

'OK, let me just shove Freda Manning back in her box under my desk and I'll come take a look with you.'

Jack's face showed the shock he felt. Not because he thought for one moment that Harrison was being serious about having Freda under his desk, but because he'd made a joke.

4

Their destination was a street in an area of Lewisham, which was on the border with Southwark. Honor Oak was named after an oak tree on One Tree Hill that Elizabeth I had allegedly picnicked under in the early 1600s. That original tree had long since gone, but another stood in its place, presiding over an area of London that had avoided the middle-class exclusivity of East Dulwich, but still retained a village feel, with Edwardian and Victorian houses lining residential roads. The historic oak had some of the best views in London; St Paul's Cathedral, The Shard, London Eye and Canary Wharf could all be seen. To the north was Nunhead and the cemetery Harrison was currently avoiding.

It had been a while since Harrison had visited this area, climbing up the hill to the octagonal viewing platform which had once been a gun mount to counter air attacks during WWI. It was said to be a hill doused in history, from the Romans using it as a lookout to spot Boudica's army approaching, to highwaymen including Dick Turpin, and a signal point for the Napoleonic Wars and then the East India Company's vessels. Could the area now be the scene of a different kind of battle, a spiritual one?

Jack drove them. Harrison had wondered if it was a ploy by his friend to spend more time alone trying to find out if Harrison was responsible for Freda's disappearance. But, as it was, they barely spoke most of the way. Harrison wasn't the most chatty at the best of times, but Jack always had something to say. Harrison wondered if his friend was angry with him; if he doubted him. Or was it concern that muted his usual ebullient character?

They pulled up in a street that was lined by terraced houses built around the 1930s. Family homes with curved bay windows constructed at a time when builders understood what a family-sized garden was, and developers weren't counting every square inch to squeeze as many houses as possible in. If only the original builders could see the prices these homes were selling for now. Harrison estimated at least three quarters of a million, and probably more. Many of the houses retained period features, such as the stained-glass art deco-style window panes on the front doors and top of the bay windows. Most had undergone loft conversions, adding to their space and value. The house they were heading to was no exception.

Drawing up outside number 18, Harrison could instantly see that it had been converted into flats some time in the last twenty or so years. A set of well-used buzzer buttons to the side of the front door indicated that four different individual dwellings lay behind its wooden entrance.

As was so often the case in multi-occupancy houses, the front garden looked much scruffier than its neighbours, with nobody feeling they had to claim responsibility for its upkeep. Harrison wondered if the landlord did much to take care of the place.

'We've not sent Forensics into the flat because we've had no reason to suspect a crime had been committed. He was a victim, not a suspect,' Jack spoke now. 'But we'd better wear gloves as a precaution. It's the top-floor flat.'

'Any word on his condition?' Harrison asked Jack's back as he pulled on a pair of blue nitrile gloves.

'Stable. I think they medically induced the coma,' Jack replied as he negotiated opening the front door. 'Not sure how long they're going to keep him in it for, but I reckon we have a day or two at least before we can talk to him.'

The two men stepped into a tired hallway, which with a little bit of TLC could be completely transformed thanks to its period features: the black-and-white floor tiles, and original decorative coving around the ceiling. Different cooking smells drifted from a kitchen in front of them. Bacon mingled with curry and boiled vegetables. Jack saw Harrison looking.

'Four flats with six tenants, two couples. They share a kitchen, but otherwise they've got their own rooms with ensuite. We've spoken to all the other residents. They've not seen anyone else coming and going from his flat apart from the landlord. At least, not that they'll tell us. Just reckon he kept himself to himself. Seemed to go out every day at the same time and they could hear him chanting, some kind of African singing, but nothing specific. He's been here around three months. We're still trying to get to speak to the landlord, see if he knows anything about his background.'

The first thing that Harrison noticed when Jack opened the door at the top of the stairs was the smell in the room. Not unpleasant, but a mix of herbs and plants which his nose couldn't untangle. Jack had stepped out of his way; he knew how Harrison liked to operate. He needed to focus, and he needed space.

For a couple of minutes, Harrison didn't move. He slowly scanned every inch of the entire room before starting to take in the details. It was sparsely furnished and the man in hospital didn't look to have many belongings. Not surprising, seeing as he was only supposed to be over for six months. There was just a mattress on the floor and no bed, which Harrison suspected was through choice. Marks on the wall at the top end were consistent with a headboard having rubbed against it, which suggested a bed had been removed. Raised beds weren't always the norm in rural African communities and it could be quite disconcerting sleeping on one if you weren't used to it.

There was a small table and two chairs, but these weren't being used for their intended purpose. Brightly coloured African robes were draped over the backs of the chairs, and the table was packed with a variety of bottles, jars, and bowls. In the furthest corner from the door was some kind of altar with a reed mat on the floor in front of it. Offerings of fruit and vegetables had been placed in a bowl. A pear that would have once been a fresh green colour was now ulcerated with black rot that leached all over the remaining fruit in the bowl. Next to them, there had been some kind of incense burnt in a pottery jug. A cluster of three dark wooden carved figures stared back at Harrison from the corner.

It all looked incongruous in what was an otherwise standard London flat. The walls had been painted a pale mocha, the carpet just a shade darker. More brightly patterned cloths had been draped over what presumably were pictures on the walls. There was no television, and the curtains were closed.

Harrison crossed to the mat and looked at a small woven

bag placed next to it. He tipped the contents onto the mat. They clunked and tumbled out. Small bones and a little piece of dark wood with white markings on it. The bones were what looked like white vertebrae and a couple of large teeth – one molar, one fang – along with some kind of coloured stones, a couple of shells, and other shards that looked like they were also bone.

Jack stepped over and peered at them, curling his nose up in disgust.

'What are those?'

'Divination bones. He will use them to speak to ancestral spirits.' Harrison scooped them back into the bag.

Next, he examined the selection of dried herbs and bottles of liquid spread across the table. Most of the bottles looked like whatever was inside of them had gone off. Dirty brown liquids and jars of ground powders.

'How did he get this lot through customs?' Jack spoke again, unable to contain himself any longer.

Harrison didn't reply. That wasn't his concern.

'Have any of these been taken away?'

'No. We gained entry yesterday after the two assailants were arrested, because it was only then that the potential murder accusation arose. We had no idea what we were looking at, so left everything as it was for you to view.'

Harrison unscrewed a jar and peered in at the contents. More bones.

'Do you think those could be human?' Jack asked, straining to see around Harrison's big bulk.

'From what I can see, I don't think so, but it's possible.'

He put the jar back down and picked up another one. Inside were dried brown pieces of some kind of vegetation.

'Devil's claw,' Harrison thought out loud.

'What? We dealing with some kind of satanic element as well as a witch doctor?'

'No. It's the name of the plant.' Harrison sighed.

Jack got the hint that he was becoming a distracting irritant, so he sealed his lips shut and backed away.

Harrison carried on, looking through the bottles and jars, sniffing and inspecting each of them. One contained what looked like black ash. Another had small pieces of a kind of bark.

By the bed was a suitcase, which he opened. It contained more brightly coloured African cloths and robes – and, more significantly, the man's South African passport was tucked into the lid. Themba Sisulu. Harrison saw the face of the room's occupant for the first time. He was a man in his fifties and the small amounts of facial hair that were growing through his dark skin had grey tips. His features showed a life that had been lived away from luxury. His hair, still mostly black, was plaited in long dreadlocks with white and red beads on the end of each strand. It was only a small photograph, but the way that Themba stared into the camera lens showed a confidence and presence which reflected his standing in his community back home.

Harrison replaced the passport and felt underneath the mattress, pulling out a pile of fresh twenty-pound notes. There was around five hundred pounds.

'We found those earlier and we're tracing the serial numbers. They're new issue so we should get an idea of where they were obtained,' Jack spoke now, judging that the information he was adding might be more valuable than another one of his questions.

Harrison didn't reply. Instead, he turned his attention to the small wardrobe, which had once been where the altar now stood – he'd previously spotted the marks it had left in the carpet. Mr Sisulu would have moved the wardrobe to place the altar in the most auspicious location for the spirits to be honoured.

When he opened the wardrobe doors, what he found surprised him. It was not clothes that filled the wardrobe, but food. Vegetables in brown paper bags. African supermarket food with brand names he didn't recognise. A wooden bowl and spoon, a metal cooking pot, and a couple of sharp knives. Clearly Mr Sisulu didn't like to keep his food in the shared kitchen, even if he had to cook down there.

Harrison double-checked all the edges of the carpet in case they had been prised up and something hidden. He then examined the curtains and the wall behind the cloths, and inspected the mattress more closely. He found nothing else.

Finally, he took another sweeping look at the room and turned round to Jack, connecting with his eyes for the first time since they'd entered the room. Jack knew this was the sign Harrison was ready.

'We're going to get the bones analysed. My worst nightmare scenario is we end up looking at something like the torso in the Thames case, boy Adam. That Themba is over here and committing some kind of ritualistic sacrifices. Anything else is going to seem like a bonus right now. So what you got?' Jack said.

Harrison shook his head. 'It isn't voodoo. Not like you'd see in South America or the movies. What did the men who attacked him say exactly?'

Jack pulled out his phone and searched for a few moments. 'They said it had been quite chaotic. There were two African women talking to the alleged victim, who was a white woman in her early seventies. The men knew her through the Catholic church they attend. They claim our witch doctor friend here, turned up raging. The women started panicking, saying the juju priest was angry, and then he directed something at the Catholic woman and told her he'd put a curse on her and her church.'

'They called him a juju priest?'

'That's what they said. The men also said that the alleged victim had told them the women were sex workers, bound by oaths which had been sworn during a ritual with a juju priest. She'd befriended them on some kind of outreach programme and was worried about them.'

'I'm not sure that this adds up. Did the men attack him then?'

'No. They saw him a few days later – the same day that the victim died after feeling unwell.'

'I need to speak to them. How did their friend die?'

'She came down with a flu-like respiratory illness. The doctor prescribed antibiotics, but she died three days later. It was an unusual illness; pneumonia usually takes longer to overcome a healthy person. She was by all accounts fit and healthy. The speed at which she died added to their belief that some kind of black magic or voodoo had been used. Of course, she may have been ill for a lot longer and just soldiered on and only sought medical help when it had got significantly worse.'

'What did the post mortem say?'

'Well, this is where we have a slight complication. She had been ill and died. A woman in her seventies. It was put down as pneumonia. There was nothing to flag it up as being an unusual death because all this was unreported until after her funeral. It was only when we arrested the pair that the whole story came out. The funeral happened, and she was cremated, so we don't have a body. You don't think he could have somehow made her sick, do you, with some of these potions he has?'

'It's possible, but I haven't seen anything that is definitely used in a negative way. Most of what he has here are plants used for traditional herbal healing. There's more to this. What we are seeing is not the real picture. We need to find out why he is here and some more details about what actually went on that day. Right now it's all smoke and mirrors.'

5

______

Their next visit was to the church at the centre of the case. St Mary-in-the-Fields.

'Looks like a mini Westminster Abbey!' Jack exclaimed as they pulled into the car park adjoining the church.

'Not sure they'd appreciate the comparison,' Harrison replied.

'Why not? Surely it's like a satellite church for their main one.'

'Westminster Abbey has been Anglican for centuries. Westminster Cathedral is the principal Catholic Church, that was only consecrated in 1910 and looks different to this one.'

'Do you know what? I don't think I ever knew there was a difference. Never been much of a churchgoer, and my parents weren't either,' Jack replied as he locked the car. 'So it's the Abbey where the kings and queens get coronated?'

'Yes.'

The two of them started to walk back round to the front of the church. A large banner, hung on the railings, caught

Harrison's eye. *Save St Mary-in-the-Fields. Donate for urgent repairs.*

'OK, tell me something, what I don't get is that surely Anglicans came after the Catholics, right? Wasn't it Henry VIII that introduced it and broke away from Rome? So how comes all the really old churches are Anglican?'

'You're right, him wanting to get divorced meant the Pope excommunicated him, but it turned out to be quite a bad business move from the Pope's point of view. Henry became head of the church in England, either took over or closed down hundreds of churches and monasteries and claimed all their lands and wealth for himself. For years after, there was a bit of to-ing and fro-ing during the reformation, but it wasn't until 1791 that Catholic worship became legal in England after over two hundred years of repression. It was only forty years later, with the Emancipation Act, that Catholics had most of their civil rights returned. That's why almost all of their current churches date from then, unless they've bought one back.'

'Do you know what? I learn something new every time I work with you,' Jack turned to Harrison, looking genuinely interested. 'How on earth do you remember all this stuff?'

Harrison shrugged. 'I spent years studying to get my doctorate.'

'Clearly more productive than my misspent youth then,' quipped Jack. 'I majored in rugby, drinking beer, and mastering *Grand Theft Auto* and *Halo* on the Xbox I'd saved all my Saturday job money to buy.'

'Gaming passed me by,' Harrison replied. He was relieved that the ice seemed to have been broken between them.

By the time he'd finished his mini religious lecture, they'd reached the top of the steps to the main entrance of the church and the air felt distinctly warmer.

They walked in through the large wooden doorway and found themselves in the church's vestibule. To their right, a rack of small candles flickered, messages to the dead from those who missed them.

'*Pray as you Go*? Are they joking?' Jack pointed to a poster on the board behind, filled with various announcements.

'Catholics are busy people too,' Harrison said. 'I think it's an app that lets you hear a prayer and bible reading while commuting. Don't forget a lot of services had to go virtual anyway during the Covid lockdown.'

'Well, as they say, God speaks in mysterious ways,' Jack added.

They walked into the nave, the main area of the church. The floor wasn't the stone so often found in older churches, but wooden parquet tiles. It lent their feet a dull thud of a walk. A vaulted ceiling with stone columns led all the way to the altar. Leading off to the sides were small chapels, heavily decorated with paintings, marble, and stained-glass windows.

There were around fifteen wooden pews on either side of the nave. Most had built-in burgundy leather kneeling pads, but the ones at the front sported brightly coloured cushions depicting crucifixes and other religious symbols. They were the most 'cheerful' element of the whole church. All around, forlorn but dutiful imagery, and marble statues of suffering saints surrounded them.

'Why is it you always feel like you should be reverent in churches? There's that vibe isn't there of piety and right-eousness? Like someone is watching you. Reminds me of being back in school and thinking the headmaster could see my every move,' Jack whispered to Harrison.

Harrison looked at Jack in surprise, half expecting him to be grinning, but he wasn't. Reverent wasn't a word he'd usually associate with Jack. He didn't have time to make a comment in return, because the Rector, Father Christopher Wilson, was fast approaching.

The rector was one of those men who would blend into a crowd if he weren't wearing the uniform of his calling: a black suit and shirt with a white dog collar. His hair was a merging of dark grey with white, and cut, Harrison noted, so that the fringe was long and combed forward. Clearly a tactic to cover the rapidly growing balding patch which had started at the front of his head. Even Catholic Fathers could be vain.

The rector gave the impression of being totally comfortable with their presence. He either had nothing to hide or was so confident in his calling that he felt safe in the hallowed protection of his church.

'The baldachin is impressive, isn't it?' he said, seeing Jack staring at the altar. 'We're very blessed to be the custodians. Catholics travel from thousands of miles away to come and see it. A true homage to our Lord because it instantly draws your eye to the centre of our worship.' The Father stopped a moment to look towards the altar and then crossed himself. 'DS Jack Salter and Dr Lane?' He half asked and half stated, holding out his hand in greeting.

'Yes, Father Wilson. Thank you for agreeing to see us.' Jack took the lead.

'If I can help in any way to sort out this awful mess, then I will be glad to,' the Father replied, 'Please come this way.'

They followed and, behind Father Wilson's back, Jack elbowed and looked quizzically at Harrison.

'The canopy over the altar,' Harrison whispered, instantly knowing exactly what Jack was confused about. Baldachin wasn't a term most people would be familiar with.

'Anne was a devout and passionate member of our congregation,' the rector said over his shoulder. 'She worked hard to help others, always putting them first. She was a sad loss to our community.'

They arrived in a small office area where an elderly woman with a pronounced dowager's hump at the base of her neck was bending over, filing some papers. The cause of her posture problems was obvious because she was lifting the paperwork right up close to her eyes and leaning forward, clearly very short-sighted. She peered at the rector and his two guests like an albino mole, squinting in the sunlight, with milky-blue eyes.

'Mrs Ricci, I think you should take a break. You've been working hard all morning, and it's time for you to go home,' Father Wilson said to her kindly. 'Thank you so much for your help.'

'Of course, Father. I'll be back tomorrow,' she replied with an Italian accent.

The three men waited as she slowly picked up her handbag, which took a little time to locate, and Harrison helped her get her coat on.

'Grazie, bello,' she said to him as he opened the door for her to leave.

'She comes here every day to help. She's been widowed six years now,' Father Wilson said to them after she'd gone. 'Unfortunately she doesn't see well, or read English fluently, so I have to find special projects just for her. It gives her a sense of accomplishment as well as the company. She hasn't noticed yet that she's been filing the same paperwork for the past eighteen months. We're pretty much all online and digital now.' He smiled at them, but there was no malice behind it. 'So what can I help you with?'

'First, we wanted to know about Anne's outreach work and the women she was helping. I understand that this was the cause of the altercation?' Jack started the questioning, while Harrison watched and analysed.

'Yes. We have several community projects, and Anne was keen to help women who frequented the streets and brothels; to help find them alternative work. Some were drug addicts, and we encouraged them to seek rehab support, but others weren't. The women who are relevant to your inquiry were African. Anne believed that they had been trafficked and were here illegally, and that they'd been forced into sex work.'

'Did you ever meet these women?'

The rector shook his head.

'No. Running a church keeps me very busy. I did offer to speak to them, and I believe that this is how the altercation happened. Anne was bringing them here to the church. She'd made tremendous inroads in getting their trust.'

'Did she give you their names?'

'No.'

'What happened that day? Did you witness it?'

'No. I'm afraid I'm not being much use to you. I only heard about it after it had happened. John Bellamy and Stephen Chase were coming in for a meeting. I understand that as they arrived, they saw Anne with the two women at the bottom of the steps. A man – she described him as a juju priest – arrived and started shouting at the women. Then he pointed a stick at Anne and our church, and the women said he had laid a curse on her and us.'

'Did Anne believe the curse was real? Do you?' Harrison asked.

'Dr Lane, as I think you may know, our Bible recognises that divination, soothsaying, witchcraft and devilry were, and still are, practised. Pope Benedict XVI highlighted that many people in Africa still live under its fear when he visited Angola not all that long ago. But I look to our current leader,

Pope Francis, who believes it is the seeds of wickedness within each of us that create the sins, not witchcraft. Those who claim to cast spells are lying and trying to control others. I suspect that view is not far from your own.' Father Wilson's eyes smiled at Harrison. 'Anne was shaken up by the altercation. She asked me to pray with her afterwards and I did so. But I do not believe that his curse was the cause of Anne's death. Her faith was strong.'

'Did John and Stephen believe it?' Jack asked now.

'You'll need to speak to them. They were upset following Anne's death. They're good men. John's wife was close to Anne and I think she's another of our congregation who hasn't been feeling well.'

'With regards Anne's illness, did it seem unusual in any way to you?'

'I'm no doctor, DS Salter. From my understanding, it was a bad flu. She had taken a Covid test and was negative. There have been so many respiratory infections around after lockdown eased. Unfortunately, this one took hold of Anne rather quickly. The antibiotics didn't seem to have any effect. Of course I didn't see her in the few days before her death as she was at home trying to recover.'

'She lives alone, I understand?'

'Yes, but I know that her friends here were checking on her.'

'Could you tell us who those friends are, please, and if anyone else might know who or where she was visiting the two African women you mentioned?'

'Yes, of course.'

There wasn't much more information they could glean from Father Wilson and so Harrison and Jack thanked him and he walked them back through into the nave.

'You're in need of repairs here?' Harrison asked, referring to the banner he'd seen outside.

'Yes, unfortunately, we have some subsidence in the rear behind the altar. If the wall slips much further, it could endanger the whole structure, and most immediately the stained-glass window at that end. John and Stephen have led our fundraising efforts and have been doing a tremendous job, but we still require a couple of hundred thousand more to secure the structure for the long term.'

'Was it totally out of character? John and Stephen attacking Mr Sisulu?' Jack asked.

'In my opinion and experience, yes. But I am sure your investigation will discover the truth, DS Salter.' Father Wilson fixed Jack with a raised eyebrow stare.

'We will miss Anne, but she has left us a bright legacy,' he added, changing the subject. 'She and some of the other ladies created our beautiful kneeling cushions. She was a talented needleworker and taught some of the other ladies, too. I think you'll agree that their bright colours add some light to our pews.'

Harrison and Jack did agree, but they wished Anne's legacy had also included her body and not just ashes, because they now had no way of knowing exactly what did kill Anne, and if her death was indeed just through catching a bad dose of flu, or if it was murder.

6

While Jack tried to track down Anne's friends from the names that Father Wilson had given them, Harrison watched the recordings of the interviews with John Bellamy and Stephen Chase. He wanted to speak to them himself, but first he'd see what had already been disclosed to the police, and what hadn't.

Both men were due to appear in court soon. They'd been transferred to Belmarsh Prison and were appearing at Woolwich Crown Court the day after tomorrow. Jack suspected they'd get bail. Harrison wanted to hear their stories before they were let back out.

John Bellamy looked exactly as you would expect an accountant to look if you went along with the cliché. His balding head shone white in the strip lights of the interview room. The last remaining hairs that clung to his scalp had been cut short to form a shadow of black reaching from one ear to the other around the back of his head. He wore glasses which were just a tad too big for his face, possibly because he had narrow features and struggled to find a style that suited him. He was a thin man, sinewy, and a little above average in height. The fact his solicitor was young and fairly athletic added a contrast to the pairing, which made John seem older than he was.

Harrison watched him as he sat in the interview room with the solicitor, waiting for the police officers to start the interview. Every element of his body language was critical in assessing what kind of man he was. His shoulders were slumped and rounded, chin and head hanging down. He was making no attempt to speak to his solicitor and looked the picture of defeat. He wasn't comfortable in this environment, which didn't surprise Harrison. It wasn't as if he was a career criminal. He didn't look like the kind of man who went into grievous bodily harm either, and there was nothing obvious in his past to suggest he was capable of it. So what had made him snap and attack Themba?

The officers who interviewed him followed the usual procedure, asking John to tell them what had happened in his own words. For the suspect, this was often the easiest part. Recount the events. To those listening, it would tell them several things. First, how well rehearsed their story was, and, secondly, give the detectives a story to pick away at, one detail at a time, to see if it all fitted together and was accurate under scrutiny.

'I first saw the witch doctor outside the church,' John began. There was clear disgust when he mentioned him, almost a lip curl and a sneer. Within seconds, John had given away a vital piece of information about himself and his attitudes.

'Anne had just arrived at the church with two women who she was trying to help. Myself and Stephen were just coming from the car park. We had a meeting with Father Wilson and wanted to pull some information together before we spoke.

This man came from nowhere, walked up to the women, and was shouting at them in their language. He was threatening. Anne looked frightened and so did the two women, who turned back and seemed to be apologising to the man. Almost begging. I heard them say to her that he was a juju priest.

'The three of them started to walk away, but he spun around and walked back up to Anne, pointing a stick at her. We were nearly up to them by now. He then said he was going to curse her, her church, and those who work with her, and that she should leave the women alone. Then he said something in his language. I shouted at him because I was worried that he might hit Anne with the stick. He held open his hand and blew something from his palm at Anne's face.

'We got to her then, and I told him to go away. I can remember him glaring at me, and then he just smirked and walked off with the two women. They didn't try to help Anne at all, after everything she'd done to help them. Anne was quite shaken up. He was very intimidating. She had this white powder on her face and clothes; it was even in her hair. I told her to go and wash it off. Two days later she started to feel unwell.'

John paused a moment, searching the interviewing detectives' faces for any indications as to what they thought of the first part of his story. Both of them were giving him their full attention, and so he continued.

'The next time we saw him was outside Anne's house a few days later. The first time it was Tuesday, and this was the Saturday evening. We'd gone round to see Anne. Margaret, my wife, needed some more of one of the coloured wools that Anne's brother had sent her. They'd been making kneeling cushions for the front pews. There's a group of them who meet regularly, but Anne hadn't been feeling well enough, so I was just getting the wool.

'We were on our way back from another meeting at the church and I was giving Stephen a lift home. The witch doctor was in the street near to her house. There's a small patch of grassland with a few trees. It's sort of a long island in the middle of the street. He was there. Had built some kind of little fire and was burning stuff like some kind of ritual. She was in there sick and he was intimidating her with his African voodoo magic.'

John paused a moment and quickly glanced at his solicitor before continuing. This next part would be critical for what would happen to him in court.

'I walked up to him and told him to leave. He asked me why and said something about spirits and ancestors. I said he wasn't welcome here, that he was being intimidating, and I tried to stamp out his little fire. It could have set the trees alight or something. It was dangerous.' John looked at the police detectives as if waiting for their agreement that putting out the fire had been the sensible move. He'd done his civic duty.

'Anyway, he jumped up then and started shouting at me. He came towards me and I thought he was going to hit me with this stick he was holding. It's hard to describe him, but he was all manic, almost like he'd been on drugs or something. He came right up to me, peering at me and mumbling something.

'I was frightened, thought maybe he was trying to put a curse on me too and that I'd get sick like Anne. I hit him in self-defence. He kind of let out a roar then and launched himself at us, so Stephen and I had to defend ourselves. He fell backwards and hit his head on the kerb. I tried to just get him to leave, but he was, I don't know he was just behaving so oddly. There was no reasoning with him. All his voodoo mumbo jumbo. I had to protect myself – and Anne.'

John stopped now and looked at the detectives expectantly. Harrison could see huge, gaping holes in his story towards the end and he wondered whether Stephen's account of the events would be the same. Before he watched the rest of John's interview, he switched over to look at his.

Where John was tall and thin, Stephen was short and overweight. Harrison estimated he was probably only around five feet seven inches and carrying an extra three stones more than his frame required. He looked less depressed and more nervous than John, but that told Harrison nothing other than the fact he was intimidated by his surroundings. His recounting of the story was pretty much the same as John's, which wasn't surprising as they'd had a few days after the attack to confer, before being arrested. There was, however, one crucial detail which Stephen seemed to remember and John had missed from his.

'The witch doctor stood up and walked towards John. He stared at him, like he was studying him or something and then he said something in African and then in English. I didn't hear it all, just a few words, *ancestors*, *love* and *protect*. Then it all kicked off.'

Harrison sat back and thought for a few minutes. Something wasn't adding up. In fact, lots of things weren't adding up. If the African priest had laid a curse, why would he go back again? The deed was done. Plus, how did he know where Anne lived? There was nothing in Themba's flat to link him to the two women, or any kind of people trafficking. There was something missing from the picture, a big hole between what happened at the church and the attack on Themba. Harrison had a hunch, but it was going to take a lot of digging to confirm it.

He finished watching the rest of the two interviews, but they concentrated on the attack and trying to determine if it was self-defence or unprovoked aggression. There were questions Harrison wanted answered – one in particular – but it was getting late, so he'd speak to John and Stephen tomorrow.

Harrison looked up Anne's address and decided to take a quick look on his way home. He wouldn't be able to get inside, but he wanted to see the area that Themba had been seen making a fire – the area where the attack took place.

Anne's road was a few streets away from where Themba's flat was located, but in that short distance it was clearly a more affluent area. Here the houses were larger, Victorian properties and the streets themselves wider. Anne lived at number 33, and as John and Stephen had described, there was an island oasis of green grass and trees, which split the road in two.

Anne's house was well kept, her garden looked after and cultivated. Harrison would have liked to get inside and get to know her a little better, but that would have to wait until Jack was with him tomorrow. She had lived alone, so in the fading light of near winter, the house looked onto the street with dark eyes. A curtain twitched in the house next door. Somebody was watching Harrison, but that was good. At least someone was keeping an eye on the place.

He crossed to the green island and searched for signs. There was no obvious evidence that an attack had taken place. No police tape or dried blood. Harrison suspected that had there been any leftover evidence, the neighbours would have been quick to clear it up and return their street to its usual peaceful haven.

Opposite Anne's house, he started to search for evidence of the fire. He expected to see scorched grass at the very least.

There was nothing immediately opposite her property, so he walked to the right, scanning the ground and bases of the trees. He suspected Themba would have chosen a place where his makeshift altar faced east and was up against a tree trunk. He walked a way along and saw no evidence, so retraced his steps and turned left from Anne's house.

He was beginning to think he'd missed it somehow, or else the men had been lying about the fire, when he spotted it. There was an area of scorched black earth, with some blackening against the tree trunk, but not enough that would have posed a risk of setting the tree on fire. A large stone had been placed in the middle. Harrison crouched down to take a closer look. Most of the evidence would have either been taken and disturbed, or blown away by now, but he might spot something.

There were a few pieces of burnt and dried vegetation, and a small fragment of cloth that looked like it was once brightly patterned. Harrison noticed the ground had a sheen to it in some areas. He touched it with his forefinger and then rubbed his thumb and forefinger together. It had an oily feel. Perhaps some kind of fat or oil had been used along with the vegetation. He sniffed it. The scent had gone, smothered by that of burnt embers and London air.

Finally, he stood up and looked around. There was nothing more to view here. Yet there was something Harrison had seen which gave further fuel to his belief that this case was not as straightforward as it seemed. He glanced at the houses across from the altar, numbers 66 and 65. He was standing quite a way from Anne's house. There was no doubt he could see it from here, but surely if Themba was attempting to conduct a ritual to affect Anne, or at the very least intimidate her, he would have been closer to her home?

Something was missing. Someone was either lying or

hiding something. Was Themba the juju priest that John and Stephen claimed to have seen? They couldn't have made up the altercation at the church because Father Wilson said Anne was shaken by it. The two women Anne had befriended were critical to the inquiry. They needed to speak to them as witnesses, but finding two illegal immigrants who didn't want to be found by the police, and were guarded by a people-trafficking ring, was not going to be easy.

7

Harrison headed home via the supermarket. He bought as much food as he could fit in his saddlebag, getting two of his favourite beef lasagnes, planning on having one tonight and to put the other in the freezer for another evening when he'd not had time to shop, and salad to go with it. He knew what it was like when they were in the middle of an investigation.

His flat was in the Docklands area of London, the top of a converted tea warehouse which overlooked the Thames. The Thames was a lot quieter now than when the building had been built in the heyday of the London docks. Then, it had been the largest port in the world. By the 1970s and 80s, the area was virtually abandoned as container ships became the main method of shipping goods, and the Thames docks found themselves redundant, unable to manage the huge ships. The buildings were left to fall into disrepair until the London Docklands Development Corporation started to regenerate the area and the city continued its relentless slow sprawl outwards.

Harrison was fortunate enough to have had a grandfather who worked in the City of London financial district, and who spotted the investment potential of these properties. He often wished his grandfather had lived long enough to see that investment succeed. It would have given him a sense of achievement, which Harrison felt he'd lacked in his career.

Harrison parked his Harley and locked it. He was just extricating his shopping from the bike, when he became aware of a pizza moped buzzing towards him at high speed. He looked up just in time to see a helmeted youth lean across and grab his own helmet off his bike seat, and promptly screech off again. It was all over in seconds. A snatch raid, which was unfortunately an all too regular occurrence in London. Usually it was mobile phones and handbags or wallets, not bike helmets.

Harrison didn't even attempt to chase him – the thief was halfway down the road before Harrison had even realised what was going on. He was annoyed with himself for not being more aware. His mind had been working through the details of what he'd seen and heard today, and not on his environment. Even more irritating was the fact he'd now lost his favourite helmet. There was only one shop in London which sold that particular brand.

Despite the fact he could easily afford to buy a new helmet, and he hadn't been personally injured in the crime, he still felt violated and disturbed by it. It was the ease with which it had happened that riled him. He had a spare – that wasn't the issue – but what he didn't want was for his helmet to end up at a crime scene if they used it in another snatch-and-grab raid. He'd have to report it just to cover himself.

Harrison let himself into his flat and felt the warm embrace that being in your own home and on safe, familiar territory provided. The last few weeks had rocked his usually solid mentality, and he found incidents like this were affecting him more than usual. He needed more meditation time to keep focused, and he was looking forward to a quiet evening in doing just that.

Harrison put Rag'n'Bone Man on his sound system, turned on the oven for his lasagne, poured himself a glass of sparkling water and headed over to his laptop to report the helmet incident.

The flat was a large, open-plan blend of modern with the old tea cargo warehouse it had once been: light wooden floors with a mix of brick and cream-painted walls. It was sparsely furnished and the cream walls carried only a few pictures of Native American people. Faces that spoke of culture, history, and life.

The other wall of his flat featured huge windows which looked out over the Thames. He found it relaxing just watching the water flow by endlessly, and while his laptop woke up, Harrison slumped into his leather armchair and stared out at the brown river. His thoughts turned to Themba and the death of Anne Francis. What were they missing?

He was just contemplating that question when his doorbell rang. He wasn't expecting anyone; he didn't give out his address to many people. Harrison instantly went into defence mode. The combination of what had been happening with Freda and Desmond Manning, and the theft of his helmet, had him on alert. Quietly, he crossed to the front door and looked through the peephole to see who was outside. What he saw made his heart jump and his stomach flip.

Dr Tanya Jones rang Harrison's doorbell again. 'Harrison, I know you're home because I saw your bike outside, and it's still warm.'

She might not be a detective, but a career working in forensics still gave her enough investigation skills to catch him out. Harrison was also aware that Rag'n'Bone Man was singing, 'I'm only human', and even if Tanya hadn't seen his bike, she'd have heard the music. For a moment, he allowed himself to marvel at how appropriate the lyrics to the song were.

Less than a week ago, he'd told her he couldn't see her again. It had been just after he'd had the flashback at Nunhead Cemetery, and his first instinct had been to cut all ties with anyone who could get hurt in the oncoming storm. He'd given her no explanation, and not even the courtesy of seeing her in person. He couldn't. He wouldn't have been able to go through with it. Now, she was here.

Tanya pressed the bell button again. Harrison opened the door before her finger had left it.

For thirty seconds, neither of them said a word. Just looked at each other.

Staring at Tanya gave Harrison the same kind of feeling you get when you arrive at a beautiful beach with a calm sea lapping gently at your toes after a long, tiring trip. That sense of serenity and beauty which washes over you and makes you want to breathe it all in and just stand and stare.

'So are you going to invite me in?' she eventually said to him.

He opened the door for her and she walked past him, her brunette hair brushing the hand that held open the door as she passed. He smelled her scent, the mix of perfume and person. It made him long to just grab her and kiss her lips. This was exactly why he'd avoided her.

'I saw Jack Salter,' she started, spinning round to face him. He could see the hurt on her face. He knew he'd done that to her. He was responsible for her pain. 'He told me about Freda in the hospice and how you'd gone to see her. Then she disappeared. He said he's worried about you. Asked me to keep an eye on you. You obviously hadn't told him you'd dumped me.' The last sentence was said with an element of sarcasm.

'I'm sorry. I was trying to protect you.'

'Protect me?'

'Yes. I believe the Mannings are planning something, something which will impact me and I didn't want to have to involve you in it.'

'So without any discussion, you just tell me you don't want to see me anymore. By text!'

Harrison wasn't sure how to answer. Behind him, the buzzer went on the oven to say it was at the right temperature to put his lasagne in.

'Have you eaten? Would you like lasagne?' he asked her, completely changing the subject.

She sighed, an exasperated sigh.

'No, and yes. Thank you.'

While Harrison quickly retrieved his second lasagne from the freezer and put both of them in the oven, he watched Tanya go over to the window and stand staring out.

He wasn't used to dealing with emotions like this. What he felt he should do, which was to distance himself from her in order to ensure none of the Mannings' poison could reach her, was not what he wanted to do. Perhaps it was time to be straight and honest. She knew some of it already. Maybe it was time to tell her all he knew.

'Would you like a drink?' he asked, walking up to stand next to her as she stood staring at the river.

'Unfortunately, I doubt you'll have a bottle of Pinot Grigio chilling in the fridge,' she replied, turning to him.

'No, sorry.'

She knew he didn't drink alcohol and so never had any in his flat.

They stood staring at each other for a few moments. There was no doubting the mutual attraction was still there. It felt like a warm magnetic pull, willing him to reach out for her.

'So, are you going to tell me what's going on?' Tanya asked him.

Harrison broke away from her and sat on the armchair opposite the sofa. Tanya settled herself on the sofa, not taking her eyes from him. She was wearing a pale pink jumper and blue jeans, and she kicked off her shoes, curling her legs up underneath her. The body language was defensive. She was making herself small so as not to be a target for more pain.

He started with the phone call from Jack and their first trip to Harrogate, while Harrison had been working away in Durham.

'I wasn't sure how I felt when I saw her,' he admitted. 'I'd been searching for them for years, hoping to get justice for my mother's murder, and yet they'd found me. Now she's dying, but I still feel that there's something they've got planned. Something which is aimed at destroying me.'

'She's an old woman riddled with cancer. What could she possibly do?'

'There are parts of my childhood that I don't remember. The time before my mother and I left for America that's just a fog. I know I was very young, but it's as though I'd blocked it all out. There's only one memory that I have. It was just before we left and it was at Nunhead Cemetery. I was there when a young woman, a friend, Annette, was murdered as part of some sick satanic ritual that the Mannings presided over.'

'Oh my God, Harrison. You were just a little boy. No wonder you were traumatised.' Tanya looked at him with a mixture of shock and sympathy.

'It's why I think my mother took us to America. She couldn't escape their cult any other way.'

'But she brought you back!'

He looked down. 'Yes. I've never understood why, but there was another revelation last week. It turns out my mentor and friend, Professor Andrew McKendrick – I think you'd have heard me talk about him?' Harrison looked back up at her. 'Well, turns out he knew my mother. I found a photograph in his desk drawer. It was of me when I was much younger, along with my mother and Andrew. All this time we've been friends, and he never mentioned it. Said it was because she'd asked him to keep an eye on me, make sure I was safe.'

Tanya thought for a moment. 'Do you think he's working with the Mannings?'

Harrison shook his head. 'No, I don't think that. I've thought about it and he's known me since I first went to university not long after my mother died, so the Mannings would have got their claws into me sooner if that was the case. But what he did tell me was that he thought my mother might have come back to the UK to help my father.'

'Oh my word, did he tell you who he was?'

'No. Said he didn't know.'

'I can understand you've got a lot to think about,' Tanya said quietly.

'I haven't told you the worst of it,' Harrison continued. 'Freda sent Jack a key to a safe deposit box. In there was a knife and part of a bloodied white dress. I think it's the murder weapon that was used to kill Annette at Nunhead.'

'Then that would prove they'd done it. Surely that's good?'

Harrison fell quiet for a few moments and looked away from Tanya. This next part was the hardest. It had torn out his insides when he'd first experienced it, and he'd dreamt about it almost every night since.

'Harrison?' Tanya pressed gently.

'I haven't told anyone about this,' he said to her, pausing a moment to calm his breathing.

Tanya nodded encouragingly.

'I had a flashback to that night in Nunhead, and I saw myself holding that bloody knife and the frightened face of my mother looking at me.'

Tanya was silent for a moment. 'So you're thinking you killed her and they'll find your DNA on the knife?'

Harrison nodded.

'I can't believe that a little boy – that you – would have murdered a woman in cold blood like that. You're the expert at this. You know how unreliable memories are. The Mannings could have planted that memory in your head, or even if it is real, they could have just got you to hold the knife to get your DNA and fingerprints on it. You were a child. Highly impressionable. And it could just be a nightmare that you're remembering.'

Harrison smiled weakly at her. 'I know you're right, and what you're saying makes more sense than what I see in my head, but you're the forensics expert and you know what it's going to look like when those results come back.'

'There are no witnesses. You were massively under age. It wouldn't even get to court.'

'But the doubt would be there – a record against my name. I don't think that's the end of it either, they've got other plans.'

'So you think you're going to get arrested for the murder of Annette once this knife has been examined?'

Harrison sighed. 'It's not so much that. It's more the fear that maybe I did do it. Andrew said that I was supposed to be their protégé, that I was deeply spiritual at that age. Perhaps they were teaching me to be like them.'

Tanya sneered. 'Yeah, or perhaps they're just evil, conniving people who were making themselves a *get out of jail* ticket and using you and your mother to achieve that.'

'But I do get angry and lose my temper sometimes. I've lashed out at suspects before.'

'Yes. You've lashed out at those who are hurting other people. You're a protector, Harrison, not a predator. Look into your own heart and tell me it's black like theirs. It's not. They're screwing with your head.'

Harrison let out an involuntary shiver of emotion. The tears that he refused to cry welled up behind his eyes. He stood up and went to the window, looking out at the brown river.

'I didn't want you getting messed up in all this, Tanya. It was a knee-jerk reaction. You'd called me just when it was all coming to a head. I just don't want you getting hurt, too. The Mannings are still out there somewhere and I don't know what they have planned next.'

'Harrison Lane, are you telling me you're worried about a pair of pathetic pensioners who aren't fit to clean your boots?'

Harrison turned back round to look at her. Tanya's face was burning with indignation and passion.

'A man with your intellect and experience should be able to run rings around them. You're not that little boy anymore, Harrison, you are far more powerful than they can ever be. They may have ruined your childhood and taken away your mother, don't let them ruin your life.'

Tanya unfurled her legs and walked over to him. He knew she was right; he wasn't that little boy anymore. His work was important, and he owed it to all the victims, like Annette and his mother, to keep fighting to help achieve justice for them.

He looked at Tanya. She was his antidote to the insipid evil that had leached into his system after seeing Freda Manning. He needed to get a grip on himself, and stand up and fight. The first thing he was going to do was reclaim his girlfriend, who was worth a thousand Freda Mannings. Harrison took Tanya in his arms and felt her body melt into his. The sound of the oven alarm telling him their lasagnes were ready didn't stop his lips from finding hers and sealing their reunion passionately. Dinner could wait.

8

It would be completely wrong to describe a man of Harrison's build and size, let alone his personality, as skipping into work, but he certainly felt lighter. That old adage, *it's good to talk*, was so true. Unburdening himself to Tanya and having a sensible and positive response back had freed him from the heavy mood he'd been in since Harrogate. She was right. He was more than a match for whatever the Mannings tried. He'd lost his usual objectivity because he was too close to the situation.

A seven-year-old's memory – even of something as dramatic as witnessing a murder – would be incredibly flawed and corrupted by age. Who knows what suggestions the Mannings had planted when he and his mother had returned from America. He'd call Arizona and speak to his stepfather Joe tonight and ask him what he remembered of that time.

Harrison rode to Lewisham police station in a much better frame of mind. He didn't even allow the large spots of rain which started to fall from the leaden sky to dampen his mood. He was due at a team briefing on the so-called voodoo case, and he needed to get on with focusing on his job and making sure the team understood exactly what it was they were dealing with.

THE LARGE, open-plan incident room smelled of coffee, canteen food, and a hint of cheesy feet and stale sweat. Full bins and a well-used tea and coffee station suggested to Harrison that at least some of them had been on a late-nighter. The team was clearly working on more than just the voodoo case – which was confirmed by a board with photographs of the remains of a heavily tattooed man, half-buried in a landfill site.

The incident room was filled with familiar faces. Harrison passed Sergeant Steve Evans first; Harrison had long ago worked out that the burly Welsh man sat nearest to the door because it meant he could see exactly who was going in and out, and when. Sergeant Evans was currently mid-way through a tense discussion with another officer about a missing torch – apparently not his first torch to have gone walkabouts. Light-fingered police officers were always in need of illumination, so it seemed.

DC David Oaks gave Harrison a big smile as he walked in. The young officer was impeccably turned out as always. Not a hair out of place, and his suit tailored and spotless. Harrison was sure he tried not to sit down too much at his desk in order to avoid getting his trousers creased.

DS Jack Salter turned around to see whom his colleague was smiling at.

'Ah, the witch doctor himself has arrived,' he greeted Harrison. 'Come to fill us in on the voodoo curse?' Harrison could see the concern hidden behind his friend's jovial façade.

'Jack,' Harrison greeted him in return.

Jack dropped his voice and stepped up to him. 'You're looking better, mate. Less stressed.'

'Well, thanks to your unsubtle hints to Tanya, she paid me a visit last night and put a few things into perspective.'

Jack gave a big grin. 'Pleased to hear she sorted you out. Nothing like an attractive and intelligent woman to take your mind off a couple of satanic pensioners.' He smirked. 'Let's get on with the briefing then, shall we?'

Harrison glanced over to DCI Sandra Barker's office on their way to the meeting room. It was dark and empty. 'No boss today?'

'She's in court. Might be back before lunch if you're still around then.'

A small contingent of police officers and civilian support staff filtered from the incident room into the main briefing room. Harrison was up first, so he made his way to the front. From here he could see everyone – and study those whom he didn't know to ascertain what kind of characters they were. He was pleased to see that diversity was really making its mark in Lewisham. Not only were there a variety of different coloured skins in front of him, but more female detectives than he'd seen before at a briefing like this.

The ratio of women hadn't gone unnoticed by Jack and DC David Oaks.

'Harrison's fan club is out in force,' Jack joked to his colleague.

'I thought everyone knew he was seeing Dr Jones?' David whispered back, scanning the female faces, who were quite obviously admiring Harrison.

'You really don't understand women, do you?' Jack replied.

'No,' David said, honestly and without regret.

'They've been after him from the moment he first came here, but he's totally oblivious and they were losing hope. Now he's seeing Tanya, he's signalled that he's interested in women and open to dating. It's all Rachel and Meera have been going on about since they first found out. You must have heard them plotting?'

David looked sympathetically at Harrison standing at the front of the room, like he was some kind of prey being stalked by a pack of lionesses.

In DCI Barker's absence, Jack introduced the briefing as soon as everyone was settled.

'OK, listen up everyone,' he started. 'We're hoping to speak to Mr Sisulu sometime today. We've heard from the hospital this morning that he's now out of the coma and doctors are pleased with his progress. John Bellamy and Stephen Chase are appearing in court tomorrow afternoon. They're claiming self-defence, but our evidence is pointing to an unprovoked attack by them. We have an eyewitness as well as some discrepancies in their own stories. I'm expecting them to be bailed, as they don't have a record and this is out of character.

'We need to find out if there is anything more to this than a straightforward revenge attack. Is it a racial hate crime? Or is there any truth to their claim that Anne didn't die of natural causes? Why was Mr Sisulu outside her house that day, for example? It's going to be tough seeing as Anne has already been cremated.' Jack's exasperation, that their key piece of evidence was now no more, showed on his face.

'However, we have several lines of inquiry. But the questions we need to ask are what could have provoked two seemingly mild-mannered devout Catholics, who are known for their community work, to attack Mr Sisulu; claiming he'd laid a voodoo curse on Anne Francis and their church? Over to you, Harrison. I think everyone in this room knows the head of the Met's Ritualistic Behavioural Crime unit, Dr Harrison Lane.'

Jack motioned to Harrison to start his section of the briefing.

'First thing I want to talk about is the voodoo element,' Harrison began, assuming that the reason most of the women in the room had leant forward and sat upright attentively was because they were focusing on what he was saying. 'There is a lot of hype and misinformation around voodoo, vodou, or voudon, as it was called. The B-horror movies featuring voodoo dolls haven't helped.

'Voudon originated in west Africa and travelled to places like Haiti, the Caribbean, and southern America with slavery. It was about worshipping ancestral spirits and, yes, animal sacrifices, particularly chickens, are made, but mostly it is not aimed at doing evil – as the movies will try to tell you. Obviously the Catholic slave owners didn't like it, so it was banned for being un-Christian.' He paused. 'Yes?'

One of Harrison's groupies, DC Rachel McGuire, had put her hand up politely.

'DC Rachel McGuire, Dr Lane,' she began as though addressing her favourite teacher. She was clearly making sure he knew her name.

Jack and David exchanged eye rolls.

'I'm a little confused, isn't Mr Sisulu from South Africa?' She looked at him with wide-eyed innocence.

'Yes. You're absolutely right, DC McGuire.'

'Rachel, please.'

'Mr Sisulu is indeed from South Africa and it was the first detail in this case that perplexed me. I'll come to him in a moment.'

Rachel smiled coquettishly at him. Harrison carried on oblivious.

'So, both John and Stephen mentioned that the two African women Anne had befriended called the man who accosted them outside the church, a juju priest. We've no reason to disbelieve that this is what the women said. Even Father Wilson used that phrase, as that was what Anne told him. This is again a west African term, particularly among the Yoruba people in Nigeria, but also in Ghana and Cameroon. These juju priests are revered in their communities. They practice traditional medicine and they are the link between earth and the ancestral spirits. Unfortunately, there are plenty of charlatans out there who haven't undergone the spiritual training and initiation and, worse still, those who use the blind belief of their people for their own ends.' Harrison looked around the room. Everyone was focused and concentrating.

'I know that some of you are concerned this might have links to the boy Adam, torso in the Thames case, the Met's longest unsolved child murder investigation. At first it was thought he was the victim of a South African muti killing. Muti is usually plants and herbs, or sometimes animal parts used for traditional medicines, but there is a very small minority of witch doctors or bad sangomas, who seek to harvest human body parts to use as muti. While this still happens, it's definitely not related to Anne's death. In muti killings, the method is brutal. The body parts are harvested while the victim is alive. The louder they scream, the better the medicine.'

A ripple went around the table at that last sentence and a couple of the officers shuffled in their seats.

'Muti was also ruled out in the Boy Adam case. They next suspected he had been killed as a sacrifice by a Nigerian cult with roots in tribal beliefs. Again, there is nothing in Anne's death that suggests this.'

Harrison paused to let all the information sink in. He'd heard a couple of the uniformed police officers talking about possible links earlier. He wanted to ensure everyone was clear about what this case was not, as much as what he believed was behind it.

'Doesn't Mr Sisulu have bones in his flat?' David asked.

'He does, but I think the bones are animal. I believe they are being tested, and the vast majority of his medicines are herbal.'

David nodded.

'Anne said she was trying to help sex workers,' Harrison continued. 'The two African women whom she brought to the church were, we believe, trafficked sex workers. Those two women are key to this case and we need to find them. There is a very well-trodden path from Nigeria to Europe, particularly Italy, of trafficked women who are put to prostitution to pay off their sponsors – those who paid for them to be brought over. In order to ensure that those women pay their debt, they are taken to a juju priest before they leave home, and made to swear an oath which involves giving up a part of their soul.'

There was another ripple around the table, this time of disbelief.

'We might find this ridiculous, but they believe they are beholden to the spirits and they absolutely have to pay off that debt in order to free themselves. If they don't, not only will bad things happen to them but also to their families. It is a belief system they have been brought up in but only a small minority of juju priests would carry out a ceremony like this. You must remember that most of these tribal priests are healers and have been key members of their communities. It is the few evil individuals, no doubt motivated by greed, who ensure that the women endure the vile conditions and treatment they have to suffer and don't try to escape.'

'You think these two women are from Nigeria and Themba Sisulu was their juju priest pimp?' Detective Constable Geoff Richardson spoke now. He was a thickset man in his late forties, with greying brown, wavy hair and a dubious choice in shirts. He liked his whiskies too, and would invariably make a pilgrimage to Scotland once a year to imbibe in more than just a few of their finest drams. Harrison had worked with him a while back and knew that Geoff pulled no punches. He said it as it was. He liked that about him.

'That's where we circle back to Rachel's question earlier. I found nothing in Mr Sisulu's flat that would suggest he was involved in trafficking or the dark side of African rituals. In fact, all the herbs and concoctions that I could see were purely for healing. He looks like a traditional sangoma or inyanga. A healer from the Zulu tribes of Southern Africa.'

There was silence in the room. Geoff's eyebrows came together in a deep frown. 'So are you saying that they are two different men, that John and Stephen are lying, or just that somebody had cleaned up the flat before we got there?'

'I don't know yet, but there are other things that don't add up,' Harrison replied.

'Jack, is this really a case for us in Serious Crimes?' Geoff turned to DS Salter. 'Nobody's been killed. Themba Sisulu is hopefully recovering and his attackers have been charged. What exactly are we investigating here?' He sounded exasperated. 'I mean, it's not like we haven't got a load else on right now.'

'We are investigating a murder allegation in relation to Anne Francis. I know we don't have a body, but what we do have is three other women, and now an elderly man who are all also feeling ill. That number is rising by the day.'

'Couldn't it be some kind of hysteria? Like Dr Lane said, if they're all so devoutly religious and believe a curse has been put on them, maybe they believe it so strongly they've made themselves ill?' Geoff questioned.

All eyes swivelled back to Harrison.

He shrugged. 'It's possible, but I would say that there would need to be somebody whipping up that feeling, spreading the gossip. I'd need to speak to those who are ill.'

'I hear you, Geoff,' Jack said. 'This was given to us because there was a fear it could either turn out to be another boy Adam situation, or it might cause racial tension. Thankfully, it's looking like the former isn't transpiring, but we do need to be able to say with absolute certainty that Anne Francis died of natural causes. In the meantime, it could still be a racial flash point, so we must be on our guard.'

'Perhaps you should get Father Wilson to have a word with her when he next speaks to his God.'

Harrison noticed that like many of them, Geoff found it easiest to lift tension and stress with some good old sarcasm and humour. He raised a few smiles around the table.

'OK, you lot, off you go. Harrison and I can go through a few more details,' Jack said to the room.

The meeting broke up with a jumble of chairs scraping on the carpet and banter about the job, lunch, or jokes about making a voodoo doll of a grumpy colleague.

Rachel hung back.

'I'm happy to help out if you need me.' She should have been addressing Jack, but her eyes were on Harrison.

'Thank you, DC McGuire. I think we can manage for now,' Jack said to her pointedly.

'Geoff's right. This is a messy case that doesn't really sit with Serious Crimes.' Jack sat back down at the table and Harrison followed his lead.

'There's something going on Jack, I'm just not sure what yet. I'll speak to John and Stephen. Find out if they're really telling the truth. I think John's hiding something.'

'OK, good. His wife's quite poorly so I'm sure he's going to get out on bail. There are two other friends of Anne's who are also not well, Jenny Ackerman and Angela Langtry. They'd all spent time with Anne just prior to her coming down unwell, and also all visited her when she was sick. It's possible they may have just caught the flu that killed her.'

'Mmhh,' was all Harrison replied. He had a hunch, but there needed to be a few more jigsaw pieces to fall into place before he could put together the full picture.

9

Harrison and Jack agreed to rendezvous in three hours so they could go over to Anne's house and take a look around. First, he needed to speak to John and Stephen in plenty of time before they had to go to court tomorrow and were released on bail.

The two men were being held in the category-A Belmarsh Prison in Thamesmead. It was one of London's newer criminal establishments, having been opened in the early 1990s, and so was better designed for modern prison living than some of the others – like the 200-year-old Brixton Prison. It also had a very handy tunnel that connected it to Woolwich Crown Court.

Modern or not, it had been a major culture shock for John Bellamy and Stephen Chase, neither of whom had so much as a traffic offence against their names to date. As a category-A prison, it held some of the highest-profile terrorist cases. It was hardly an average Sunday's Catholic congregation.

DC David Oaks volunteered to accompany Harrison to

the interviews. He needed a police officer with him just in case something was said or done that could be admissible in court. DC Oaks had jumped at the opportunity. The pair of them borrowed a pool car and headed over to Woolwich.

The journey took around half an hour, heading through Blackheath and the open air and green space of Greenwich Park. Past the Woolwich Ferry until they were finally upon the vast area that was once part of the former Royal Arsenal in Woolwich and now contained three prisons. Belmarsh, the privately run Thameside, and the youth offenders' institution, Isis.

'Always thought that naming the young offenders' prison, Isis, and it being right next to where the terrorists get put, was quite prophetic,' David mused as they drove past a sign.

'Yeah, it's a shame that the name has become tainted with a link to fundamentalist terrorists.'

'Why did they call it that?'

'Isis? It's the ancient name for the Thames. There was also a goddess in ancient Egypt called Isis, but now most people think of the militant jihadist group, the Islamic State of Iraq and Syria.'

'Strange how language evolves and words come to mean different things over time.'

Harrison threw a glance at David. He was clearly feeling extra philosophical today.

THEY'D ALLOWED time to get through the process of showing their ID and being checked for any illegal items. Harrison had been here before, so he knew the drill, and DC Oaks was used to prison visits, even if it was his first time at Belmarsh.

They were shown to an interview room, and John Bellamy was brought in by a guard.

He looked as if he'd been locked in a dark cell for weeks. His skin was definitely paler, leaching dark shadows under his eyes. It was as though he'd rejected all colour and become a gray-scale shadow of his former self. His face was more drawn, and he was less defeatist and more anxious today.

'I thought we'd done all the interviews. I'm due in court again tomorrow. We're applying for bail,' he said the minute he came into the room.

'I appreciate that you've spoken to my colleagues, Mr Bellamy, but my name is Dr Harrison Lane – I'm a psychologist and I work with the Ritualistic Behavioural Crime unit. I've been asked to look into what happened not only to Mr Sisulu but also Anne Francis.'

At the mention of Anne's name, John looked genuinely sad.

'She was murdered, that's what, by that witch doctor's curse. He cast his evil onto her and to my wife and the others.' He became more animated and Harrison could see the vein in his neck pulse.

'Before we carry on, you are aware that you can have a solicitor present?' He checked.

'Yeah. It's fine. I've got nothing more to say that will make any difference.'

Harrison studied John's face for a moment, allowing the man's features to register in his mind so that he would be able to spot any subtle changes.

'How long had you known Anne?' Harrison asked gently. He was fishing now. John's response had told him something, and he needed more.

'Six years. We met through the church when Margaret – my wife – and I moved here from Bristol. She was so welcoming to us both. Amazing woman. She'd do anything for anybody. Worked tirelessly to help those less fortunate.

Always full of life and smiles. It's wrong, just wrong, that she was targeted and taken from us. I wasn't even able to go to her funeral because I was stuck in this place.'

Harrison watched John's face closely. When he talked of his memories of Anne, it had brought a smile back to his lips and a light in his eyes. As he focused once more on her death and its cause, the scowls had returned.

'I'd like to ask you about when the attack happened. You were driving to see Anne, I understand?'

'Yes, that's right.'

Harrison already knew it was because he'd listened to the interviews from before, but he wanted to hear John talk about it again. He gave a small nod of encouragement.

'Margaret needed some more of the wool that Anne's brother had shipped over to her. They were making the kneeling cushions with it and so they wanted to ensure they used the same wools each time. Anne was really quite poorly by this time. She died just a few hours later.'

Harrison nodded sympathetically.

'You saw Mr Sisulu outside Anne's house?'

'Yes, he was there blatantly doing his black magic rituals, burning some kind of offering. He could have burned the bloody tree down. How did he get her address? He must have been stalking her.'

'Was he right outside Anne's house?'

'Yes. Well, not quite directly outside, but very close by.'

'So you confronted him?'

'Yeah, of course. I got out of the car and tried to put his damned fire out first, and he started mouthing off in his African language. I told him to leave. He came right up to me, threateningly. Probably trying to put one of his black magic curses on me, but I said a silent prayer in my head to our Lord. His voodoo magic wouldn't be able to hurt me.'

'I understand he said something to you, something in English?'

John looked away from Harrison now and disengaged. He shrugged.

'Something about love, ancestors, and protect?' Harrison pushed.

'It was nothing. I didn't understand him. He was in my face by then. I felt threatened.'

Harrison readied himself for the big reveal.

'Did he, by any chance, intimate anything about your relationship with Anne?'

John Bellamy did an excellent impression of a rabbit caught in headlights teamed with a confused chicken. He looked wide-eyed and searched around the room in all directions for somewhere to look other than at Harrison. He also seemed to flush in embarrassment, at the same time as having the colour drain from his face.

'What? That's preposterous. I'm a happily married man. Anne was a friend, that's all. She's my wife's friend. I can't believe that you are suggesting such a thing. I'm a devout Catholic, you know.'

'Mr Bellamy, the vigour of your denials, and your general body language when talking about Anne, show me that you did indeed have feelings for Anne. Mr Sisulu may not have mentioned Anne by name, but I think he believed he saw something in you, and you interpreted that as being about Anne.'

John went to protest again, but Harrison held his hand up.

'I'm not accusing you of having an affair, but I'm just saying that you were very fond of Anne and this fondness may have clouded your judgement.'

John didn't reply. Harrison took that as a *yes*.

'Which leads me on to asking, how sure are you that the man you saw outside the church that day is the same man you saw outside Anne's house?'

'I'm one hundred per cent sure. It was him, both times. We don't get many witch doctors wandering around London, you know. It was the same man. Dreadlocks, bright African-print clothes.'

'Could you identify him for me? I haven't yet met Mr Sisulu.'

John frowned at Harrison, clearly not convinced about why he was being asked the question. Harrison took six photographs out and laid them on the table in front of him, one by one. All of them were passport-style photographs of black African men. Three had dreadlocks, three had short hair.

'This some kind of trick? Are you trying to catch me out?'

'No, no. I'm just asking you to identify the man you saw outside the church and who you got into the altercation with.'

John scowled again, but looked back down at the photographs.

'I'm not sure. Definitely not any of these three,' he said, pushing the three short-haired men back at Harrison. 'Could be him.' He pointed at one of the pictures, squeezing his eyes together in concentration.

'It might help if you close your eyes a moment and think back to the times you saw him,' Harrison offered.

John looked at him and then did as he'd suggested. He closed his eyes for around thirty seconds and then re-opened them and looked back at the three photos. He shook his head.

'It's been stressful being in here, you know. I'm not

thinking straight. It's really hard to sleep. The noise, banging, and my cell mate snores.'

John looked again at Harrison and back down at the photographs.

'You are definitely discounting these?' Harrison pushed the three short-haired men towards him again.

John looked at them and then nodded his head.

'Absolutely certain. I think this is the guy, but like I said to you, I'm not sure now. I need to get some rest so I hope you're not going to hold me to this. Use it as evidence or something?'

'It's OK, Mr Bellamy, it was for my reference. Thank you.'

Harrison collected up the photographs, putting the one John had chosen at the top.

'Just a couple more questions, Mr Bellamy. Did Anne believe the witch doctor had put a curse on her?'

'She was concerned, Dr Lane. I don't know where you are in your faith journey, but I know the devil and his evil are real forces in this world. Anne's faith was strong, but if that man was doing the work of the anti-Christ, he could have infected Anne and others in our congregation with his evil. He blew something into her face. Something that he conjured up in his palm. We don't know what that was. My own wife is now ill, others from our church are falling sick. What more proof do you need, Dr Lane, that some kind of curse has spread its infection through our midst?'

'Thank you, Mr Bellamy. I think that's all I need to ask you today. Thank you for your time.'

John nodded and stood up.

'God looks after the righteous, Dr Lane. I trust in him that justice will prevail.'

· · ·

As soon as the interview room door had shut behind him, DC Oaks let out a big breath. 'Woah, that was heavy!'

'Never forget the power of faith,' Harrison said to him.

'What was the purpose of asking him about the photographs?' DC Oaks asked. 'We know who he attacked.'

'I wanted to see if he could identify Themba Sisulu.'

'Can I see? Did he choose right?'

'No, he didn't.'

Harrison handed over the six photographs. The one that John had chosen was of a black African man in a brightly coloured shirt with dreadlocks.

DC Oaks put it on the table at the top and then placed the others out underneath it. 'But, isn't this the same guy as that one?' He pointed to two photographs that John hadn't chosen, one of a man with short hair, and one of a man with dreadlocks, but wearing a suit.

'That's correct, DC Oaks. Well done. You passed the test. Both of those photographs are in fact of Themba Sisulu, taken from his passport photograph and photoshopped. David failed to identify him, or even see that there were two of the same man.'

'What does that mean?'

'Do you remember your witness training?'

'Yes... Well, I think so.'

'OK, then you should remember that eyewitness misidentification is the most common cause of miscarriage of justice.'

David nodded, concentrating on what Harrison was saying.

'Did you notice what John said when I asked him if he was absolutely sure that the man outside the church was the same man as outside Anne's house?'

'Yes, he said something about it being extremely unusual

to see a witch doctor with dreadlocks and bright clothes in London.'

Harrison nodded. 'He was identifying the clothes and hair, but not the face. The man he chose out of my very unscientific identity parade was an African man with dread-locks and a bright top. With very few exceptions, we are generally poor in our facial recognition skills at the best of times, but we are also heavily biased towards faces we see all the time. Research has shown we're far better at recognising faces from our own age group and our own ethnic groups. It's a fact, for example, that white people are more likely to incor-rectly identify a black suspect.

'I have serious doubts that Themba Sisulu was the same man who stood outside of their church and laid that curse on Anne. I can't tell you yet why Themba was near to Anne's house, and I have no idea who the original man was, but I definitely think that John Bellamy attacked the wrong man. Question is, who was the juju priest and did the powder he is alleged to have blown into Anne's face cause her to be ill, and is that illness now spreading?'

10

Harrison and DC Oaks spoke briefly to Stephen Chase, following their chat with John. The conversation added nothing to what they already knew, but he too failed to identify Themba from the photographs, and instead went for the same man as John.

Harrison was buoyed by the knowledge that he was on the right tracks with something, but it had opened up even more questions and avenues of inquiry. He was eager to get back to Lewisham and find Jack so that they could head to Anne's house. Perhaps he would discover some answers there.

Jack was out of the office when Harrison got back, but news of the photo ID parade experiment had spread around the incident room, and, by the time Jack returned, Harrison was surrounded by a small group of highly attentive police officers. Almost all of whom were female.

'Psychological research indicates that we recognise faces in a totally different way to other things. That's why we see face patterns in lots of bizarre and random objects. It's believed to be the area of the brain called the fusiform gyrus, which is activated when we look at faces. We simply don't have the vocabulary to describe individual features of a face, which is why the old method of photofits were so unreliable. You must remember that even asking a witness to provide a verbal description of the suspect may make it harder for them to ID them later. It's called verbal overshadowing, where memory is harmed by rehearsing information.'

'That's just so interesting,' DC Meera Kapadia said.

'It is indeed,' said Jack, interrupting the gathering, 'but unfortunately, you're going to have to book in another time slot for your next psychology session, because I need Dr Lane with me now. We have criminals to catch and I thought you lot were all flat-out busy.'

'THEY'RE like bees to the honeypot with you,' Jack muttered to Harrison.

'What do you mean?' Harrison asked him.

'You don't really think they were all crowded around you just to hear about our fussy gyros, or whatever they're called in our brains, do you?'

'I was under the impression they wanted to learn more about the eyewitness identification of suspects,' Harrison replied, totally innocently.

Jack sighed. 'For one of the most astute men I've met when it comes to crime scenes, you are completely clueless about women.'

Harrison looked decidedly miffed.

'Come on, let's go and have a look around Anne's house. Get you away from your fan club for a while.'

As they drove to Anne's house, Harrison filled Jack in on his conversation with John Bellamy.

'Great, so the list of people we're hunting has increased, and we're still no closer to working out if Anne was in any way attacked by this mystery juju man. Do you think the powder he used could have done something?'

'It's possible, but it doesn't explain why other people are now falling ill.'

As they drove up Anne's street, Harrison had a good look at the houses along the road. Why would Themba Sisulu be making an altar here? What ritual was he performing, and why? If it wasn't for Anne – and that was quite possible seeing as he wasn't right outside her house – then who was it for?

Ryan was back in tomorrow: he'd get him working on it. Finding out who else lived in the road might give him some more clues.

'So, Anne Francis,' said Jack as he opened her front door, 'is what they would have once called a spinster. Never married. Never had any kids, and has just one family member; her brother, who is a missionary in South America. Both devout Catholics.'

'He get over for the funeral?'

'No. Apparently, one hazard of the job for missionaries is that they are often in very inhospitable places with poor modern communications. Unfortunately for us, Anne had left instructions that Father Wilson should make the arrangements for her funeral. Had they waited for next of kin to deal with it, we would still have a body as evidence.'

The two men stepped into a neat, but decidedly chintzy, hallway, which was a melding of floral imagery with Catholic icons. Pink flowery wallpaper and a delicate-pink carpet were teamed with a picture of the Virgin Mary and the baby Jesus.

Harrison felt it was a somewhat gaudy image – not the most delicate he'd seen, but each to their own.

Jack stooped to pick up some letters which had gathered on the hall mat. The mat read *God Bless You* in large red letters.

'Mostly bills and a couple of Catholic charity begging letters,' Jack said, looking through the envelopes. He put them onto the hall table with the others. Both of them had already donned the required blue nitrile gloves and over-shoes to prevent contamination.

While Jack searched through the rest of the post, Harrison walked through into the front room. It was another melee of flowers and religion. Anne's overarching preoccupation with her faith was evident everywhere. Even the cushions on the sofa carried religious imagery and slogans.

Harrison's eyes ranged around the room.

'She obviously wasn't that into TV then,' Jack said, joining him, and motioning over to the corner where a bulky old-style cube TV sat. It looked so dated, retro, compared to the flat-screen TVs which now graced most living rooms. The small screen housed in a bulbous-backed black plastic casing looked many decades old, rather than something which had only ceased production at the beginning of the 2000s.

'Liked her music, though,' Harrison added. A large book-case was taken up with row upon row of CDs and topped by two speakers. Just a short way away was an old-fashioned deck system on a shelf. It had a record player on top, then a CD player and even a cassette tape player and radio.

'I guess if it ain't broke, why chuck it. That's what my parents would say,' Jack commented. 'They've still got their old sound system too.' He wandered over and looked through the CDs. '*Christian Hits of the 80s, Greatest Hymns, My Savior,*

Top 50 Praise Songs. Doesn't look like there's any chance of a bit of Motörhead or Def Leppard in her music collection.'

'No. It looks like Anne lived her life as she said she did: a devout Catholic.' Harrison looked at the photograph of the Pope on the mantelpiece. The only other photographs in the sitting room were a black-and-white image of an elderly couple, presumably her parents; and a colour photograph of a man dressed in a priest's cassock, with semi-naked South American native people crowded around him, looking totally incongruous. Presumably her brother.

'I'll go upstairs and leave you to look around down here,' Jack said, mindful of Harrison's need to be alone.

Harrison waited until Jack's feet had reached the top of the stairs, and then he stood in the middle of Anne's living room, breathed in deeply, and focused his mind. He needed to understand who Anne Francis was. Would she have convinced herself that she was cursed and somehow her own mind had shut her body down and caused her death? It wasn't unheard of. Or were they really looking for something that just wasn't there? An unsettling experience with a pimp, a bout of the flu, and a friend or perhaps admirer who wanted to be her knight in shining armour? On the face of it, that's what it looked like, and yet there was something else that just didn't fit for Harrison.

Once he felt fully grounded and focused, Harrison began to look in detail around the living room. He searched for signs that somebody else had been looking before him. He looked for hidden meanings in everyday objects, and tried to get a feel for who Anne Francis really was.

He sat down in the sunken armchair that had a footstool, an electric radiator, and a small table and lamp next to it. This was where Anne spent her time when she was in the house. In front of him was the Pope and a large wooden crucifix attached to the wall above the mantlepiece. At his feet was a bag with brightly coloured wools and a kind of rough canvas, where Anne had been making her next kneeling cushion. Religion was Anne's life. She lived to serve her God.

Harrison carried on around the rest of the house. The kitchen was next. Here he found Anne had a penchant for Marmite and pilchards, although maybe not together. Her recycling bin was filled with empty pilchard tins, and there was a stack in the cupboard. She must have eaten them nearly every day – probably on toast, if the mouldy loaf of bread was anything to go by. There were no mass-produced breakfast cereals, just a large Tupperware tub of porridge oats. She lived a frugal life. There was little in the way of excess, and no alcohol to be seen.

'How you doing?' Jack asked, coming into the kitchen.

Harrison shook his head. 'Nothing we don't know already.'

'Well, apart from her stash of wool – she's got a massive bag of it upstairs, sent from South America. Maybe she was some kind of contraband wool dealer or knitting addict,' Jack joked, opening up the fridge and recoiling at the smell of sour milk and rotting vegetables.

'It was needlepoint rather than knitting,' Harrison corrected. 'She made the kneeling cushions in the church.'

'I have no idea what the difference is,' Jack replied absent-mindedly.

'Needlepoint is more like embroidery. You sew the wool onto a type of open-weave canvas.'

'OK, thanks!' Jack said, but Harrison could tell he was more interested in Anne's dietary preferences than her needlepoint.

Upstairs, Harrison looked out of Anne's bedroom

window. It was at the front of the house and, from here, he could see a lot of the street both ways. To view where Themba had been conducting his outdoor ritual required him to push his forehead against the glass, and only then could he just about see the area.

He looked at the bed in which Anne had died. It had the look of a sick bed; several used glasses and tissues on the side, and the sheets were well-creased. Behind him, Jack came into the room.

'Who found her?' Harrison asked.

'One of her friends, Angela Langtry. They'd been taking it in turns to come in and check on her, shared a set of keys that Anne had given them for that purpose. Anne was dead in her bed. Medics found nothing untoward. Actual cause of death was probably heart failure.'

Harrison nodded and wandered into the spare room, which was dominated by the big bag of brightly coloured wool that Jack had mentioned. It was enough to make an entire church full of kneeling cushions, and he suspected that was the intention. Some of the packaging was still attached and he could see the South American postal stamps.

Jack absentmindedly followed him and stood out in the hallway, waiting.

Harrison found a bundle of postcards, one of which was of an African scene. He looked through these, searching for any signs that Anne may have known Themba or had some connections. They were all from friends who were either on holiday, at retreats, or lived abroad. He guessed that she probably cultivated pen friends. Perhaps there was some Catholic scheme she took part in, connecting with like-minded individuals around the world. Harrison continued his search. There had to be a clue somewhere in this house.

. . .

BEHIND HARRISON, Jack's phone rang in his pocket. He fished it out, but didn't recognise the number.

'DS Jack Salter.'

'DS Salter, we have a note on the system to notify you in connection with any incidents relating to Freda or Desmond Manning.'

Jack looked over at Harrison, who was still sifting through some letters and postcards. He showed no signs of having heard the conversation, and Jack quickly walked out the room.

'Yes, that's correct.'

'I'm calling from Putney MIT. We've got two deceased individuals who we've identified as Freda Louise Manning and Desmond Warwick Manning. It was a poor attempt at making it look like an accident. We're treating it as a double murder.'

11

Patience woke up to the sound of fists battering at the front door of their flat and a woman's voice screaming for help in Nigerian. She was in the pitch dark – there were no windows in her bedroom to see by. Patience jumped out of bed and hit her leg on the wooden wardrobe in the tiny room. She cursed. She was disorientated. The room stank of grease, which cloyed at every pore in her skin, suffocating it. The fish and chip shop downstairs vented its deep-fat fryers into the narrow alleyway they shared outside and somehow the fumes found their way into every room in their tiny flat.

The screams from outside got more desperate and now she heard a man's voice. Patience knew what to do. She ran to the tiny kitchen and grabbed a glass bottle from the side and then rushed to the front door in her bare feet.

Patience scrabbled with the lock. She was shaking, so her fingers were clumsy. She heard a crunch and then a heavy thump against the door. As she flung it open, Florence fell backwards into her, and then to their hallway floor, her face already covered in blood. The source of her injuries almost fell in on top of them both. The wide-eyed white man just managed to right his balance and stand up again to face them, ready to give Florence, and now Patience, a dose of his anger.

Patience knew what was coming. She'd been here many times before, and she didn't hesitate. Holding the bottle by the neck, she smashed it against the wall just outside their door and then lunged towards the man with the jagged broken glass. It grazed his cheek before he could jerk out of her way.

'You bitch!' he shouted at her, rubbing the back of his hand across his face and finding blood.

'Come on then,' she said to him, waving him towards her. 'Come, try me and see what else I give you.'

The man weighed up the odds. In front of him, the crazy black woman stood firmly in the doorway of the flat, the other whore at her feet behind her. She was stirring now too, coming round from the punch he'd given her.

The one holding the bottle looked strong. She was solid and muscular, and she had a firm hold of the glass bottle in her right hand. For a few seconds, his mind went back to his original mission for that evening, and he wished he'd had her for his £15 worth and not the other one. His eyes strayed to her breasts, which strained at the long T-shirt she wore. His anger was draining back down to his penis. Then a noise down the corridor told him someone else had been woken by the rumpus. The bitches weren't worth it. He turned and ran.

Patience winced as she took her weight off her left foot and brought it up to her right knee. The piece of broken glass she'd trodden on had sliced into the sole of her foot. She pulled it out and immediately blood poured from the wound.

She'd clear the mess up later. First she had to check how badly he'd knocked Florence around.

Limping, Patience dragged her friend further into the flat by holding her under her armpits. Florence groaned in pain. Quickly, Patience shut the door, putting the double lock back on. It was still dark. She'd not had time to turn on any lights, so she stepped over her carefully and flicked on the switch.

Florence moaned as the light flooded her face. Patience's heart sank. It was clear the man had given her far more than one punch. She'd been subjected to a beating, probably while she was trapped in his car, or up against a wall in a doorway or alley.

They faced that risk every night. Each time they took a new client, they had to weigh up the odds. How much had he been drinking? What kind of man was he from the clothes he wore, or how he spoke? What was his car like? Some of the richest men were the worst; nice cars didn't necessarily mean nice people. When business was slow, the danger was that they got less picky. The need to earn had probably made Florence more reckless. She was lucky to have made it home.

Patience had been there before. When it happened, they thanked the spirits for looking after them and making sure they weren't killed.

Florence would give thanks to her ancestors for tonight's deliverance, but not yet. First, Patience would help her bathe the cuts and try to reduce the swelling.

Tonight was going to cost Florence: no punter would pay for a woman who looked like she'd done ten rounds with Tyson. A tear trickled slowly from the corner of Florence's eye, diluting the blood that still seeped down the side of her face.

'It is a test, my sister,' Patience said to her gently, 'tears will do no good.'

As she gently washed Florence's face, Patience started to hum a song that they sang all the time back home in the state of Edo, southern Nigeria. It reminded her of being outside under the shade of a tree in the African sun. She missed her mother and sister, she missed her aunties and the village gatherings, but she didn't miss the poverty and the endless days when she longed for something better.

What they had now was hard, but it was temporary. In another three years or so, they would have paid the madam what they owed her, and they would be free of the vow. Then, Patience could stop this work and find another job. Maybe cleaning, or cooking. She liked cooking. When she had decided to make this trip, that's the job Madam's man in Nigeria had told her she would get. *Cook to a nice family in a big London house,* he'd said to her.

She had fallen for the web of lies, the dream he'd woven. She'd thought that maybe things might not work out so perfectly, but this reality was far worse than anything she'd worried about. Just a few more years and she'd be free of her debt. Able to send more money home then. Her parents would be proud of her.

Patience turned her full attention back to her friend. Florence had talked of working in a beauty parlour. She wanted to paint the nails of rich women with soft hands, and Patience could remember the little manicure kit that Florence had carefully packed for their journey. It never made it to Europe.

Florence's job in the nail salon hadn't existed. The only clients she saw were men.

Patience turned Florence's face to the side and looked at the cut on her cheek. It had split the skin and there was dirt on it. She'd probably done it when she fell to the floor in the doorway, or maybe he had hit her to the ground earlier. It was a bad cut.

Patience would do the best she could for her with what they had. There would be no hospitals, they'd been warned by the madam when they first arrived. They were illegals, which would mean instant repatriation to Nigeria. She would have to return home, having broken her vow to repay her sponsor. That would mean bad luck for her and her family. She would be cast out by her parents and cursed by the spirits for the rest of her life.

Whatever happened, they would have to stay hidden. She would also need to keep going out and doing her job in order to pay Madam. This was their life now, and she just had to hope the man didn't come back for more.

Jack told himself that not telling Harrison about the phone call was because he was protecting him. In his heart, he didn't really believe that. He needed to go and view the crime scene for himself, alone. Dark thoughts were infecting his mind. First Freda disappeared after Harrison had visited, and now this. Could there be any possibility that his colleague and friend was responsible? He told DC David Oaks he had to go out and interview one of Anne's friends. It wasn't a complete lie. He'd got an appointment booked in for that evening. He was just massaging the details.

FREDA AND DESMOND spent their last few hours of life a long way away from the fresh air and natural landscapes of Wales where their cult had resided all those years ago. Their last moments were in a damp, mould-ridden house that was due for demolition, on the outskirts of Putney.

It surprised Jack how nervous he felt when he arrived

outside. He was desperate for the doubts in his mind to be driven away by whatever faced him beyond the fluttering police tape that cordoned off the property. The Mannings must have a lot of enemies, he reasoned with himself. They'd allegedly killed at least two women that he knew of, and, according to Inspector Rob Morgan, who'd been with the Carmarthen police at the time, they'd dabbled in all sorts of blackmail and coercive behaviours. Not to mention their satanic side. It was easy to suspect Harrison because he had a motive. It didn't mean he was capable of doing it.

The street was a hive of activity. A fire engine was parked up directly outside the house, and the evidence of the fire that they'd been called to put out was easy to see. Blackened window frames in the downstairs still dripped with water from the torrent that had been used to dampen the flames, and the stench of smoke and soot left an acrid, burning sensation in his nose and throat.

The fire crew were rolling up their hoses and checking equipment. They'd be gone soon, to be replaced by a fire investigation team once everyone was one hundred per cent sure that no pockets of fire could have escaped their notice, and their equipment was safely stored and checked, ready for the next job.

Jack wasn't surprised to see a fire investigator was already on scene, the back of her red London Fire Brigade bib carrying the words: *Fire Investigation Team*. She was in the hallway talking with the forensics officers – two white-suited individuals, fully masked and covered, ready to record everything they could in amongst the devastation.

Jack suited and booted himself too, and gratefully accepted the mask offered – although it was unlikely to protect him from the stench of smoke. The smell would sink into his clothes and hair despite the protective suit, and he'd have its remains in his nostrils for the rest of the day.

The police officer in charge of signing everyone in and out of the scene called his boss, who quickly appeared from the darkness of the building, squeezing past the three forensic experts in the hallway.

'Cotton top!' An officer in his early forties walked towards Jack with a big smile on his face. He had curly brown hair, cut short to control the waves, and brown eyes which looked too soft for the job, but Jack knew otherwise.

Jack groaned. Not because he wasn't pleased to see the man, but because of the nickname. 'Well, if it isn't Detective Inspector Gordon "the Gopher" Jacobsen.'

Gordon Jacobsen had worked with Jack in Lewisham for years until he'd transferred out about eighteen months ago. Jack liked the man. A solid investigator and generally a good all-round bloke, apart from his choice of nickname for Jack. The name had come about because early on in Jack's career, the investigating team had been sitting around a table and Gordon had commented how Jack was the only blond in the room. *Like a cotton top in a field of thistles,* he'd said. Since Gordon transferred, Jack had worked hard to eradicate the nickname from living memory. He'd even resorted to bribery, persuading two colleagues to constantly and vocally call him *Salty* around the rest of the team so that it stuck. He'd just about succeeded in that battle.

'How's Lewisham? And, more importantly, I hear you're now a daddy.'

'Good, mate, thanks, and yes, Daniel's coming up to a year old soon.'

The two men shook hands heartily, and Gordon clapped Jack on the back.

'Congratulations, he a cotton top like his dad?'

Jack resigned himself to the nomenclature. 'He is, as a matter of fact. Blond and blue-eyed. How's life in Putney?' Jack knew Gordon had got divorced. He'd never had children, and the divorce had been the catalyst for the transfer.

'Same old shit with work, but got myself a good woman. Can't complain.'

'Well, thanks for alerting me to this,' Jack said to him, nodding at the house behind.

'I understand it relates to a case you're working on?'

'Yes, a historic murder case.'

'I hope you'll share any information that might be pertinent to our inquiry here?' DI Jacobsen queried, and his soft eyes hardened a little as he studied Jack.

'Absolutely, of course I will. Total disclosure, we've got no reason to hide anything.' Jack conveniently put Harrison out of his mind.

'OK, good. So, fire brigade responded to an anonymous 999 call at 7:35 a.m. They arrived to find the house on fire. No immediate signs of life, but on entering the building, they discovered the bodies of two individuals, who we have since identified as Freda and Desmond Manning. Initially, it was suspected to be an accident, there are a lot of drug-users who frequent this area, but the fire crew quickly decided that an accelerant had been used and at least one of the victims has evidence of tape around her ankles and wrists. Let's go through now, and then I'll finish up once you've had a quick look. We can only go so far obviously as Forensics are still combing through, but it will help you to understand what we think may have gone on here.'

Jack followed DI Jacobsen inside the dark building. It had been an absolute tip before the fire, but now wasn't going to need too much encouragement when it came to demolition time. The epicentre of the fire had been in the living room, off to the left of the hallway. The entire room was black and anything remotely combustible had turned to charcoal. Gordon stepped to one side of the doorway so that Jack could peer in.

'The first body is to the right, not much left to recognise it as a human being, but it was once; and the second body, which we believe to be Freda, is on the left, just underneath the window.'

Jack looked to his right. A charcoal facsimile of a twisted human shape lay curled on the floor. The body must have been doused in petrol or some other accelerant, because it was at the centre of the blackest hell hole. It looked as though if you nudged the shape, it would disintegrate. His mind was already racing ahead. Getting DNA from that was going to be impossible.

To his left, the blackened window frame held no glass. Even before the fire, it had probably been smashed and cracked by a succession of vandals and squatters, but there were some fragments of glass from where the fire crews had finished the job for them. The glass lay shattered on the floor underneath the window, but some of it was on top of what was definitely recognisable as a human being. Jack thought back to his and Harrison's visit to Freda Manning at the hospice in Harrogate. He could just make out her wasted body shape. It certainly looked like her.

'The fire crews came through the window,' Gordon explained needlessly. 'And also entered via the door. They were able to bring the fire under control quite quickly.'

'Excuse me.' The fire investigator slipped past Jack in the doorway, closely followed by the two white-suited forensics officers.

'OK, let's get out of here,' Gordon said to Jack.

Jack was more than glad to comply. The smoke was still

strong enough to burn his lungs. The forensics team had on proper masks with filtering; his served only to make his face hot.

The two men walked out of the front door and through the front garden of the property. It had clearly already been covered in rubbish; now detritus from the fire and investigation littered it further. The investigation team would have to be careful while sifting through the house and garden: they'd need to be wary of used needles.

Jack and Gordon pulled off their forensic suits and walked across the road where the air was marginally fresher and a breeze could fill their lungs with what passed for oxygen.

'So, tell me about Desmond and Freda Manning,' Gordon said to Jack. 'I've already looked on the database and neither have criminal records. The only alert that came up was to contact you.'

'Well, they're not your cuddly pensioner types,' Jack started, watching with bemusement as Jacobsen took out a packet of cigarettes and lit up. Replacing one type of smoke with another. 'Thought you'd given up?'

'Yeah, well, you know how it is.' Gordon dismissed Jack's concern.

'They ran some kind of satanic cult in Wales during the 1990s. We have them as prime suspects in a cold case from 1993 in which a woman was murdered in some kind of satanic ritual or sacrifice. There are also suspicions about a recorded suicide at their cult camp in 2004. We think they were into blackmail and extortion, but they'd been hard to find until only a few weeks ago, when Freda Manning turned up at a hospice in Harrogate.'

'Hospice?' Gordon's eyes narrowed. 'That fits.' He pulled out his mobile phone and scrolled through some photographs, before turning it around and showing Jack. The image was of a hand, relatively damage-free, lying among the blackened rubble in the house.

'Her hands are fairly intact. The fire didn't reach them. You'll see the bruising on the back of it, and the mark where a needle has been. That's probably where a canula was inserted. Was she very late stages? Cancer?'

'Yes,' Jack confirmed, and Jacobsen nodded.

'So how did she end up here?'

'She went missing a couple of days ago. Just disappeared from the hospice without a word.'

'So, we could be looking at kidnap and murder, all premeditated, and sounds like there might be a few candidates who'd like to see them dead.'

It was Jack's turn to nod. He swallowed hard and tried not to think of Harrison, as though the other officer could somehow hear his thoughts.

Gordon dropped his cigarette onto the pavement and ground it out with the heel of his shoe.

'How did you identify them?' Jack asked.

'In the kitchen, we found Freda's handbag and a jacket that belonged to Derek with ID in it. That's his car, we're just waiting on the truck to pick it up.' He nodded towards an old maroon Volvo estate a little way down the road. 'Obviously we can't be sure yet. Are they on the DNA database?'

Jack shook his head. 'Get on to Harrogate, they'll be able to supply you with Freda's fingerprints and some of her DNA from the hospice. I presume Derek's car will be full of his, but again that's not irrefutable.'

'No, but we're tracking down their last known address. The car isn't even registered to Derek. We are trying to ascertain if that's a false name, or it's actually somebody else's car.

He had the key in his jacket pocket, which is how we found it.'

'And you're sure it's murder?'

'Yeah, as I said, Freda's wrists and ankles were both tied with tape. Keeping our fingers crossed that we find something on the tape. I love that sticky stuff.'

'What about the 999 call? You said it was anonymous?'

'Yup. No idea at present. We're trying to trace it, but it could have been a druggie with a burner phone who didn't want to be identified.'

'Mmmh.' Jack's mind was whirring.

There were lots of convenient aspects of the scene, and a few inconsistencies. He wished he could have brought Harrison in to take a look. It might not have been ritualistic, but Harrison's tremendous analytical mind would have seen things that they often missed. And yet Jack couldn't let him anywhere near the scene. Harrison was compromised. Too close to the Mannings to be a part of an investigation like this. Also, and most importantly, he might well end up being a suspect and so he needed to keep him well away from where Harrison could accidentally leave his own DNA or fingerprint traces.

13

Jack headed back to the office with a thousand questions spinning around in his head. It wasn't good to be emotionally attached to a case, but he was. In reality, he should hand this all over now to someone else, step back from the Mannings, because his relationship with Harrison could totally compromise his investigative abilities. He wasn't going to, though. He'd started this, and he'd damned well see it through.

Knowing that Gordon Jacobsen was Senior Investigating Officer on the fire gave him some confidence. At least Jack knew they'd work well together. He couldn't say that about every team outside of Lewisham.

The minute he walked into the incident room, he was jumped on by DC David Oaks.

'Been in touch with the vice team and I've got a lead for a potential brothel that uses Nigerian sex workers. It's only a few roads away from Anne's church.'

It dragged Jack back to the investigation he was supposed to be concentrating on.

'Great. If we can find those women, we'll get a lot of answers. I need a coffee so I'll meet you in the car park in ten.'

It turned out that Jack needed a lot more than just a coffee. As soon as he arrived in the canteen and saw what was on offer, his stomach reminded him he hadn't eaten in hours. It resulted in a slight over-calculation of just how much he could eat, but he figured David would hoover up any spares.

David was already sitting in the passenger seat, waiting, when Jack got to the car park. 'Bloody hell, how much are you eating?'

Jack plonked his entire haul onto David's lap.

'Oh my days! Don't mess the suit!'

'Help yourself.' Jack smiled at him. 'Except for the Cornish pasty. That's got my name on it.'

'I'm fine thanks, had a Caesar for lunch.'

'Salad?'

'Yeah. I can't do a ton of carbs like you. I'd bloat like a hippo.'

'You serious?'

David looked serious.

'You youth these days,' Jack said half-jokingly, but he meant it too. At David's age he'd have thought nothing of consuming two pizzas in one sitting.

They pulled out of the car park and headed to the address David had put into the system, accompanied by the sounds of a Cornish pasty being consumed.

'How's your dad doing?' Jack asked, in between mouthfuls.

'He's getting there. Gone back to work part time now, which is good.'

'They're doing a ton of research into Long Covid, so hopefully the doctors will get on top of it soon.'

David nodded.

'I hope so. We're lucky his doctor's really good, but it's been a nightmare few months. Mum's lost over a stone with the worry.'

'I'm not surprised.' Jack's mind jumped to when he too had been totally distracted and worried about his wife, Marie, and their son, Daniel. It hadn't been Covid which had threatened his family, but post-natal depression. Over the last year, he'd come to realise just how important health was.

They drove in silence for the rest of the way. Partly because both of them were thinking about sick relatives, but also mainly because Jack had his mouth full of various items of food. By the time they'd arrived, he'd polished off most of his haul. David had succumbed to an apple turnover, which Jack thought was a token effort. Both men brushed the crumbs off themselves as they got out of the car and prepared to enter the alleged house of ill repute.

Jack wondered how David was going to fare over the next few minutes. He remembered his own first encounter with a pack of prostitutes. His cheeks hadn't stopped burning for hours afterwards, and he'd felt so uncomfortable that he'd never forgotten it. He hadn't blamed the women. A lifetime of servicing men and often getting abuse at the same time gave them some rights to ridicule and tease them.

The first thing that Jack noticed was that it didn't technically look like a brothel. It wasn't a seedy massage parlour where you could get extras, run by a pimp or Madam who did very well out of desperate women trying to earn enough money to get by.

The two detectives climbed the stairs to the walk-up, a drop-in for sex. A sign on the ground floor advertised: *Models, Come on Up*. Jack knew the reality wasn't going to meet the expectation, but suspected that most of the men who had made this climb knew that. It was only a short walk to the first floor, where Vice had told them they'd find three flats being used by sex workers.

At the first door, Jack rang the bell. Its shrill tring could be heard inside, but it wasn't met with any response. David walked ahead and rang on the second door. He got lucky.

An Asian woman in her forties answered the door. She was one of those women who looked insignificant and small, but had a core of strength, both physically and mentally.

The second she saw David and Jack, she tried to shut the door again. David had anticipated this and was too quick for her. The look of pain on his face as his foot got crushed, looked like he regretted the move.

'Please, we're not here to bust anyone. I just need some information.' Jack saw David still wincing with pain and pushed at the door with his shoulder. He held up his hands as if to surrender. 'Really, I promise. We're not Vice.'

'Layla, Layla...it the rozzers,' the woman shouted back into the flat.

'What now?' was all they heard, followed by a pair of stiletto heels thumping across a hardwood floor. 'This is harassment!' A young woman in her thirties, with a face like thunder, appeared at the door, and her maid melted back into the flat.

'Honestly, we're not here to harass you. We're just trying to find some women who we believe have been trafficked from Nigeria. I just want to show you a photograph, ask a couple of questions, and we'll be on our way. I give you my word.'

'You've got five minutes and if I miss a client or you scare one off, you're paying.'

Jack didn't hesitate. He pushed the door open and he and David entered the flat. It was nicer than either of them had imagined it would be. Some of the furnishings Jack recognised from Dunelm and Primark, but it was all quite tasteful. A small purple sofa and chairs were arranged around a glass coffee table.

Through a door, they could see the maid taking sheets out of the washing machine and feeding them back into a tumble dryer. She pretended to be busy and ignoring them, but Jack could see she had one eye on them all the time. That was her job. Clean, do the admin, and help look after her employer. She was Layla's eyes and ears. If something got too rough, you can be sure she'd be ready to deal with it.

'Your lot have tried to close us down countless times. You'd rather we were out on the streets where we can't look out for each other and stay safe, and yet you expect our help.' Layla sat down on the purple sofa, exhibiting her long bare legs underneath the silky dressing gown that left little to the imagination.

'Like I said, we're not Vice. We investigate murders, Ms...?'

'Just Layla to you.'

Jack could tell she wasn't convinced. Layla scowled at the pair of them like a caged animal, wary that at any time they might spring a trick on her. She was a bottle-bleached blond with an enhanced cleavage and a relatively fit figure. She might not have made it onto the books of Elite or one of the other modelling agencies, but Layla was a fairly attractive woman and presented herself well. She was certainly in a different league to the needle-scarred girls he saw on dark street corners.

Layla had some pride in her profession, and while she might do some recreational drugs for all he knew, she didn't look like an addict. She wanted to stay alive and safe. He had some sympathy. Brothels were illegal, but a woman having sex in her own flat wasn't. As long as they didn't advertise their services and a third person wasn't benefitting from them, they were technically not breaking the law and, like she'd said, it was a lot safer. There'd been a recent court case when the police had tried to close down some walk-ins, only to have it overruled by the courts. It was no surprise they were met with hostility when they came to ask for a favour.

'An African man is alleged to have murdered a woman after she tried to help two Nigerian women who claimed to have been forced into prostitution.'

Jack had slightly inflated the murder angle, to show they weren't there from Vice.

Layla used her tongue on the roof of her mouth to make a loud tutting noise. 'You lot are always using sex trafficking as an excuse to come in and raid us.'

'No, really, I have no interest in shutting you down. I merely want to know if you've seen any African women who are being managed by an African man and are under duress. It's a safeguarding issue.'

'They're unlikely to be walk-ins. You're more likely to find them on the streets or in managed premises.'

Jack knew what she meant by 'managed premises', but it was a somewhat misleading term. There were two kinds: the brothels where prostitutes worked and a pimp or madam managed them, fed them their drugs, and took most of their money; and then there were the worst kind, the ones where the girls were held captive and punters were brought in to effectively repeatedly rape them. The traffickers tended to run those.

'Any particular streets or premises?' He tried his luck, not expecting anything in return.

Layla shrugged.

Jack pulled out the photograph of Themba Sisulu from his jacket pocket.

'You ever seen this man?'

She peered at the photograph, raising her eyebrows and shaking her head.

'Nope.'

'Definitely not?' Jack tested, watching her closely.

'Definitely not,' she replied, looking him straight in the eyes.

The doorbell rang.

'Time's up, gentlemen. You either ship out or pay me for my time.'

'We'll go. You're absolutely sure you've not seen these women?'

'I'm sure.'

Jack and David started to make their way back towards the door.

'Not that way. You'll scare off my client. You two go in there until Tina tells you it's OK.'

Layla opened the door to a spare bedroom. Jack and David obediently stepped inside. They listened as Tina opened the front door and greeted a man, chattering away to him. It didn't take long for the transaction to take place, and the man and Layla retired to the rear bedroom.

The door opened, and Tina called them forward, holding open the front door. Neither man said a word until they were back in the corridor.

'Well, that was a waste of time,' Jack said.

'Do you think she's being honest?'

'Yes, and no. I think what she said makes sense. The women we're looking for are more likely to be lower down the pecking order, hidden. This place is higher profile. Too risky if you're an illegal. These girls here work for themselves. We're looking for an organised ring that is controlling women and doesn't care about their welfare. Who was it you spoke to at Vice?'

'Terry Dukes.'

'Mmmh, I'm wondering about Layla. I think she's a smart woman who probably not only knows more than she's letting on, but also knows a lot of people. It wouldn't surprise me if word now spreads that we're looking for these women.

'I think Vice has just used us like a pair of Jack Russells. Relationships have broken down after they tried to shut the walk-ins and failed. We're here to rattle some cages and flush them out, so our colleagues in the vice squad can then go in for the kill and claim the prize.'

14

Jack was annoyed that he'd wasted his time being 'played' by Vice. It was the end of the usual working day for most people. Traffic had built up and getting back to the station was a slow and frustrating process. Harrison had come back into his mind. He was going to have to confront him about Putney. Jack was just dreading seeing a reaction that gave away anything other than total surprise.

It had been a long day, and he felt drained. After nearly fifteen years in the force, he recognised it as emotional tiredness. As a police officer, like the other emergency services, you had varying impacts on your psyche. There was the physical nature of the role; although as a detective now, the job didn't involve chasing and battling to arrest suspects to the same degree as the uniforms, but he'd still been on his feet a lot of the day. Then there was the mental tiredness. Concentrating for long periods, trying to interpret evidence and memorise every detail you could because you never knew what might end up being important. Interviewing suspects meant being on constant alert for every tiny sign that could give something major away.

Finally, there was the emotional side. You learned to separate yourself from the victims as much as possible. If you didn't, then the job would destroy you quite quickly. It wasn't that he didn't care. He did, and some cases still found their way inside, but you needed to develop a degree of separation from them to be able to view the crime objectively.

Today it was a rarer form of emotional exhaustion. It was the kind you got if a colleague was injured or killed on duty. This time it was because he was worried one of his colleagues might have gone off the rails and murdered two people. He needed to speak to Harrison.

THEY WERE STILL a fair way from the office when David took a call.

'It's the hospital. Themba Sisulu is awake. They said we can go speak to him.'

Jack stifled a sigh. He'd been hoping to clock off.

'Do we need an interpreter?' he asked, pulling himself together.

'She's not sure. He hasn't said a word yet. Seemed to think he can understand them, but probably safer to have one.'

'OK, let's just use the Language Line app for now. We can always bring someone in tomorrow if the more personal touch is required. Let's go see what he has to say.'

Jack did a few manoeuvres to adjust their direction. He'd far rather be heading home at this point, but, with any luck, the interview wouldn't take too long.

As soon as they arrived at the hospital, he texted Marie with an estimated ETA for his return. She knew he liked to see Daniel before he went to sleep, so they'd agreed that if she knew roughly what time he was coming, she'd do her best to have him ready for bed but still up to say goodnight. On the extra-long days, he had to make do with just a kiss on his son's sleeping face.

Themba had been transferred into a small ward with some other men. They found him lying on his back in bed, as still as a stone carving. As they walked towards him, Jack could see his eyes were closed, but the second they got within a couple of feet, they shot open, almost giving him a fright.

John Bellamy had given Themba a good going over, with the aid of Stephen Chase. Themba's left eye was swollen with a small suture showing that there had once been an open, bleeding cut just to the right underneath his eyebrow. Dark bruising showed through his natural skin colour, and there were other cuts on his upper lip and cheek. He was a man who didn't carry an ounce of fat on him at the best of times, but lying in the hospital bed, he looked positively wasted away. The trauma to his body had clearly drained it.

The nurse who accompanied them gave a brief condition update. 'Mr Sisulu is refusing to eat and drink. He also hasn't spoken since he woke up. We have the psych doctor coming to see him.'

Jack nodded and wondered if it was trauma or guilt that kept his lips sealed.

'Mr Sisulu, I'm Detective Sergeant Jack Salter, and this is Detective Constable David Oaks from the Metropolitan police. We're here to help you. The men who attacked you have been arrested, and we will prosecute them for what they have done to you. But if we're to take this case to court, we need you to answer a few questions for us. Would that be OK?'

Themba Sisulu gave no signs he was hearing Jack, let alone listening to him. He stared straight up at the ceiling.

'OK, let's try Language Line.'

Jack repeated his introduction, and they listened as the interpreter on the other end spoke in what they hoped would be Themba's native tongue.

Themba stayed motionless.

'We're assuming he's not deaf?' David said to Jack.

'John and Stephen said they had a conversation with him. He can hear and he can certainly speak some English. For some reason, he's choosing not to.'

The two of them persevered for another ten minutes, trying a couple of other potential dialects via the app, in the hope that something would spark a connection.

'Mr Sisulu, we understand you have had a traumatic time. We can't help you if you refuse to speak with us.'

No response. Not even a flicker of his eyelashes.

Eventually, Jack gave up. On their way out, he spoke to one of the nurses. 'Have you managed to get him to say anything?'

She shook her head. 'Not a word. We get no response at all from him. He just lies there staring at the ceiling or with his eyes closed. We've got him on a fluid drip to keep him hydrated, but that can only be a short-term measure. We're working on it.'

'WELL, that was another waste of time!' Jack said to David as they got back in the car. 'This case is going nowhere fast.'

'We've had an email from Father Wilson,' David said, reading from his phone. 'Another two people have fallen sick. Not direct friends of Anne's, but elderly regular worshippers.'

'Maybe we should advise they call in Public Health. This could be some kind of rogue killer flu spreading. Last thing we want is it to turn out to be the epicentre of the next pandemic. I'll speak to him in the morning.'

JACK'S MOOD was not in a good place. Not only was this investigation frustrating him – he didn't even know if they had a murder case at all – but the spectre of the Putney fire scene and its ramifications were hanging over him. He decided to call it a night, and after dropping David off, he headed home.

As he neared his house, Jack remembered the time he used to dread the moment he arrived in the neat, modern close of family homes. Theirs was a semi-detached property with an integral garage. He glanced at the lawn. The grass was covered in autumn leaves, blown over from the next-door neighbour's tree. He'd clear those at the weekend. Maybe they'd get snow this year; the thought of taking Daniel out in it and building a snowman in the garden filled his mind and brought a smile to his lips. He wanted to be sure the grass was clean so that the snow stayed pristine white even when you rolled it up into a giant snowball. In his head was an image of Daniel's bright little face with rosy cheeks, wrapped up in the padded all-in-one suit they'd bought him a week or so ago.

A few months ago, he would have been terrified of what he might find behind the front door that he now pushed open. He'd been so worried about Marie and the toll that the post-natal depression had on her. He'd also been worried about Daniel. It had taken time, love, a visit to her parents, and eventually the doctor, to help break the cycle that she had become stuck in. Now she talked openly about her struggle and spoke to professionals as well as her friends. Most importantly, she'd also now bonded with their son.

It was the sound of this bonding which greeted him when he stepped into the hallway. A crescendo of hysterical giggles were coming from upstairs. Jack stopped still and just listened. Daniel must be in the bath because there were splashing sounds, interspersing the giggles, and noises of faux protest from Marie. He didn't want it to stop. He stayed still, allowing the giggles to wash over him, drenching the day's worries and disappointments. Was there anything more addictive and healing than a baby's laugh?

Eventually, he climbed the stairs to join in the fun. Marie was kneeling by the bath, and a red-cheeked Daniel was inside it, with some plastic contraption that he was using to splash his mother. At Jack's approach, they both turned around.

'Dada!' Daniel squealed.

Marie grinned. She was soaked. Her hair was wet, and the top she was wearing clung to her and dripped with water, but she had the widest grin he'd seen on her face in the longest time. Jack stood there and looked at them both, grinning back.

'What on earth have you two been up to?' He laughed.

'I wouldn't come in here if I were you,' said Marie, 'or the whale will squirt you with his spout.'

Jack clocked the plastic whale in Daniel's hand.

'Oh he will, will he?' He was darned if these two were going to have all the fun. Jack stripped off his jacket, tie, shirt and trousers, dropping them to the floor where he stood and then stepped into the bathroom to join in the water fight. He didn't bother that his socks soaked up the pools of water on the bathroom floor. His soul was replenished.

15

T he small Asian woman was hidden from view, wrapped up in a big black padded coat that almost doubled her size. Perhaps it was a deliberate ploy; hide her identity and make herself look bigger at the same time.

She peered out from between the hood and zipped-up neck of the coat: only her eyes could be seen as she passed the street lights. She was nimble on her feet, despite her middle age, and she seemed able to move around the pavements, weaving in and out of tourists and shrinking away from CCTV cameras, like a shot of mercury.

There was nothing mercurial about her mind. She knew where she had to go and who she had to see, and there would be no stopping her. Layla had been clear with her instructions.

If she was honest, Tina didn't like the woman she was about to meet. Didn't like her methods or her business model. She was sure Layla didn't realise the extent of the woman's empire and those who were trapped within it, but love can be blind and it wasn't her place to question.

Tina knew she'd arrived at the right place because the letter boxes on the peeling flat doors were all sealed up, and there were locks on the outside. It was a long way from their neat, bright Soho flat, but not that great a distance away.

The woman was waiting for her. She looked at Tina as if she'd stepped in her on the pavement, and Tina was glad she wasn't younger. The advantage of middle age was that you started to become invisible to some people. She preferred it that way.

She passed on the message. There were no questions, no reaction, and no thanks. The woman simply turned her back on her and made a phone call. She'd soon be moving them all on to new premises. With any luck, she'd move much further away and so she'd call things off with Layla, but Tina doubted it. Layla had eyes and ears in places the woman could only dream of: she was too useful to lose.

Silently, Tina turned and slipped away, not wishing to stay there any longer than she absolutely had to. Job done.

16

Harrison was about to turn off his office computer and head home when a hesitant knock came on the door. He didn't need to tell them to come in because the visitor immediately tried the handle and pushed the door open, revealing a tall, distinguished-looking Black man in his sixties.

'Harrison. I was upstairs, thought I'd see if you were in.'

Their conversation was decidedly hesitant for two men who'd known each other and been the best of friends for over fifteen years.

Professor Andrew McKendrick walked in, studying Harrison's face for any reactions to his presence. He was smartly dressed, as always. Harrison recognised Andrew's tie as one of his regulars. It was the navy silk one with red stripes and a crest of King's College University at the bottom.

'I'd not heard from you. Wanted to be sure you're not avoiding me,' Andrew said to him.

Harrison sighed and looked at his old friend. 'I've had a lot on.'

'Is that the only reason?'

Harrison hesitated, thinking about how he was feeling. He'd always been honest with Andrew. 'I won't pretend that finding the photograph wasn't a shock. It was. I don't understand why you never told me you'd known my mother.'

It was Andrew's turn to sigh. He suddenly seemed older and looked for a chair to sit on. Harrison stood up and cleared some magazines from the spare chair by his desk. Andrew took it gratefully and slumped down into it.

Harrison waited for his old friend's explanation as to why Harrison had to find the photograph of Andrew, his mother, and him as a little boy, in his desk drawer. Andrew had never, not in all the fifteen years they'd been friends, mentioned that he'd known them back when his mother was alive.

'If I'd have told you right from when we first met, do you think we'd have become friends? I think you'd have tagged me as some stalker who was keeping an eye on you, and you'd have avoided me. I'm damned sure that if I was in your shoes, that's what I'd have done. You were already incredibly wary after what had happened in Wales and so I thought it was for the best.'

Harrison didn't reply, just let Andrew carry on.

'Once we'd been friends a while, I never found the right time or way to tell you. After that, it was too late. I was worried I'd get exactly the reaction you've exhibited since you found out. You now don't trust me. I promise you that I've never had anything but your best interests at heart.'

Andrew paused a moment, trying hard to swallow the constricting band of emotion which was around his throat. 'I don't have any kids, you know that. You're the closest I've got. At first I kept an eye on you as your mother had asked, then it was because I wanted to for your sake, and yeah maybe selfishly for my own.' Andrew hung his head.

The air between them was heavy with emotion and unspoken words which drifted in from the years gone.

'So tell me about my mother,' Harrison said, 'were you in love with her?'

Andrew nodded.

'She was easy to fall in love with. She embraced life and had no thought for social conformity and the need to follow some ready ploughed route. It was exhilarating being in her presence. You know how much I loved my parents, but generally they lived a very conformist lifestyle. I think they felt the need to do so for me – you know, because it was so unusual then for a white family to adopt a Black child. Perhaps they thought they could somehow make me fit in better if I followed every societal norm there was going.' Andrew smiled ruefully.

'So, your mother was a breath of fresh air, but there was also a vulnerability about her. She was almost too fragile for this world. They saw that, the Mannings, and they preyed on it at first. When she came back from America, she was different. Stronger. It was as if she'd found her purpose in life. I think it was the need to protect you which changed her.'

'Joe helped us, too. He was good for her,' Harrison added.

'I think you're right.'

Harrison's mobile phone rang and vibrated on the desk in front of them. Both men looked at it.

'You answer that. I have to get going, anyway. Only popped in quickly after a meeting upstairs. Please don't be a stranger, Harrison.'

Harrison gave a small smile and lifted his hand in goodbye before answering the phone as his friend slipped out of the office.

'Harrison, it's David Oaks, DC Oaks. Jack has asked me to

give you a call to see if you can meet up tomorrow morning first thing for a catch-up.'

'No problem, what time?'

'8:30 a.m. at Lewisham, that OK for you?'

'Fine.' Harrison replied. He briefly wondered why Jack hadn't rung or texted him himself, but didn't dwell on it. He'd find out what was going on in the morning.

As HARRISON PULLED up outside his flat, he was reminded about what had happened the previous evening, and the fact that he'd not reported the theft of his helmet. Tanya's visit had completely thrown him. The minute he got in, he walked over to his laptop and logged the incident. He also needed to remember to get a new helmet. He had plenty of incentive: he and Tanya had talked about getting out of town one weekend and he'd need a spare for that.

Harrison sat back a few moments and the memory of Andrew coming into his office filtered into his head. He looked at the clock. It was just gone 6:30. In Arizona time, that would be just gone 11:30 a.m. It would be a long shot as Joe might still be on shift, but worth a try. He picked up his phone and dialled America.

He always considered Joe his stepfather, even though Joe and Harrison's mother had never married. They'd spent around seven years together, and they'd been the best years of Harrison's life.

He had no other father besides Joe, and he couldn't have asked for a better example of one. Joe was not only a good, kind man, but he was one of the most experienced of the Shadow Wolves, the elite Native American trackers who help patrol the American/Mexican border for drug smugglers. Joe lived in an area that belonged to the Tohono O'odham

Nation, and there Harrison and his mother found a spiritual home, as well as a physical one.

Joe had taught Harrison everything he knew about tracking and survival, as well as the essential skill of observation. Harrison had gone to school, but the most valuable lessons were always the ones when he got home and was able to head out into the desert with Joe. Out there, the two of them connected to their environment in a way that made him forget who he was.

Joe shared the benefits of what he called the sacred silence: meditation that allowed him to banish all distractions from his mind and focus. He also showed Harrison how to balance his spiritual self with his logical, scientific mind. At that age, Harrison hadn't recognised the conflict these two created within him, and what Joe showed him became the philosophy he lived and breathed to this day. It was the basis of his work: understanding the power of belief and spiritual need in people, but being able to observe those who used it to hurt and injure. He owed Joe a lot.

Harrison's heart lifted when he heard his voice answer the phone.

'Joe, it's Harrison,' he said, aware of the smile that crept onto his lips, despite the fact Joe couldn't see it.

'Ba'ag,' Joe greeted him. It meant eagle in Tohono O'odham, which had been Harrison's spiritual animal name.

'Good to hear your voice,' Joe continued.

'How are you?'

'We are good. The work, it's the same. A big haul last week, and Stella has made principal.'

'That's such good news, please congratulate her for me.'

Stella, Joe's wife, was a teacher. She was as gentle and patient as Joe was, although Harrison knew Joe could also be a ruthless hunter if required and suspected that Stella could also hold her own if faced with a difficult student.

'And you?' Joe asked now.

Harrison sighed. He wished he was there with Joe in the Sonoran Desert, in Arizona. He could imagine their dusty homestead, about fifty-five miles southwest of Tucson. He could even smell the desert if he closed his eyes and took himself back there.

'It's been a tough couple of weeks, Joe,' Harrison said, and told him about the Mannings. 'I also had a flashback, a memory. It was before we came to America. Mum and I were witnesses to a human sacrifice. Did she ever speak of it?'

'No. Your mother never spoke of the time she spent with the Mannings. All I know is that there was a reason why she left.'

Harrison felt a flutter of disappointment. It was always like this, brick walls whenever he asked questions about the past. He paused a moment, gathering the courage.

'I saw myself with a bloody knife, as though it was me who killed the victim.' His voice trailed off.

'It is bad spirits who put those images in your head, Ba'ag.'

'But you don't know if it's a real memory or not.'

There was silence for a moment as Joe thought carefully of what he wanted to say. 'You came to me with a troubled heart and mind. I saw the dreams you had. Something haunted you, at first, both day and night. Then the dreams came only on bad nights. I don't know what went before. I knew only the boy who lived with me. I saw your soul. It was wounded, but when you left, it was whole again. You were strong. You had a deep spiritual connection that I'd never seen before in a child. It allowed you to see what others couldn't.

'You still have that gift and you use it for good. What happened in the past has gone. You must cleanse your mind, Ba'ag. Clear those thoughts which try to poison your soul and destroy your focus.'

Harrison hadn't got the answer he'd been hoping for. Joe was the one man who could have known what happened at Nunhead, but it was another dead end. Yet Harrison also knew that Joe was right. He had allowed his mind to become infected with bad dreams. He'd allowed himself to get so wrapped up in the hunt for the Mannings, that he'd lost control of his focus and rational thought.

Tonight he would regain that control, ground himself again as Joe had suggested. Cleanse his soul the way Joe's ancestors would have done. He prepared himself for a smudging ritual in order to clear his mind and restore harmony. He would exorcise the Mannings from his psyche.

HARRISON STRIPPED naked and prepared a space in his living room area to sit and meditate. He wouldn't eat tonight. He needed to focus on more important fuel for his body.

First, he opened one of the windows. The gasp of cold air that came in to his flat reminded him he was alive, prickling the skin on his chest and sending a shiver down his spine. He turned off all phones and his laptop. It was important that he gave this his full focus. All electric lights were switched off. There was nothing but the bleeding white glow of the Docklands around his flat, and a thin pale moon straining to be seen above the city's light pollution.

He gathered together the herbs he would use for smudging: sage, cedar, and sweetgrass and placed them, wrapped in a tobacco leaf, into a clay bowl. Then he settled himself on some cushions on the floor, drawing his spine up straight and breathing from his belly. Big, deep breaths filled his torso with air. His abdominal muscles tightened and rippled in the pale shadows, while his powerful shoulder muscles flexed and contracted as he prepared to merge flesh and spirit.

Harrison lit the dry herbs, which flamed up quickly. He allowed them to burn for around thirty seconds before extinguishing the flames. Now the smoke came. Rising up from the bowl.

He picked up a large golden-brown feather. It had come from an eagle which once soared above the desert in which he'd spent his childhood. Then, bending over the bowl, he wafted the smoke around his head and body, closing his eyes and clearing his head of everything but positive thoughts. All around him, the ancient eyes of Native Americans looked on from the portraits on his walls.

He sat in silence, working deeper into the meditation. Slowly, he began to reclaim his inner strength, rejecting the evil that had tried to sap his energy in recent weeks.

A powerful urge began to rise from the pit of his stomach. His breathing grew deeper still, sucking the poison from his insides, until finally it was ready to burst from him. He was barely moving and yet Harrison's whole body gleamed with the exertion, every muscle taut and ready. With one final deep breath, an animal roar escaped from him, expelling his anger, doubts, and fears.

He flexed his biceps and pectorals and clenched his fists. He was ready to fight.

The thin trail of smoke wafted through the air and out of the open window, taking the negative energies with it. Tonight he would sleep well. Tomorrow he would be strong enough to take on anything the Mannings had planned for him.

17

Jack felt guilty about the fact he'd got David to call Harrison about the meeting in the morning, but he couldn't trust himself not to blurt something out. He wanted to tell Harrison the news in person, not over the phone. He had no idea how Harrison was going to react, but as a friend and a police officer, Jack wanted to be there.

Unusually for him, he didn't fancy breakfast this morning. Instead, he was up early. Leaving Marie and miraculously Daniel both sleeping, he crept out of the house and was in the office before a quarter to eight. He'd never been an early riser by choice, but once up, he loved the relative peace of a new morning. It never failed to give him a sense of fresh beginnings. A renewed start to the world.

Jack went to the canteen for a coffee and took it back to his desk so that he could go through his emails before the rest of the team arrived. He wanted to see if Gordon Jacobsen had sent an update on the fire scene. He was delighted but not overly surprised to see that he had. Gordon always was an efficient bugger.

Morning CT

Not too much to report yet, but initial indications are that Freda Manning was given a massive dose of morphine, which would have meant she was dead before the fire was set. Waiting on further indications as to how long before. Will keep you informed.

Thanks for the historic info.

Gordon

It gave Jack some relief because that indicated something important to him, but he only had a couple of minutes to digest the information before the doorway to the incident room was filled by Harrison Lane.

Jack wasted no time. 'I'm just going to have a few minutes alone with Dr Lane,' Jack said to the sergeant coordinating the morning briefing. 'I'll let you know when we're done.'

Jack deftly guided Harrison straight through the incident room, avoiding walking past the desks of known groupies who were starting to congregate ahead of the briefing. He didn't have time to waste, and he needed to have this out with Harrison. It reminded him of that feeling he used to get before a big talk with a girlfriend he knew he wanted to dump. Trepidation and anxiety, because he had no way of knowing how they were going to react.

With Harrison inside the meeting room, Jack closed the door behind them. Harrison sat down in one of the chairs and looked at him, a little puzzled.

'Everything OK?'

'I have something to tell you, or maybe that should be something to ask you,' Jack fumbled his words. He'd been practising how he was going to deal with this, but he had never quite managed to get it right. So, in the end, he just blurted it out. 'Freda and Desmond Manning have been found dead.'

Jack watched for Harrison's reaction. He'd been sitting back quite relaxed in the chair, but shot bolt upright at his words.

'Both of them? How?'

'Suspected murder. I've got to know, Harrison… If you had any part in this, you must tell me. I know who's investigating this, and he's no slouch.'

Harrison stood up now and paced the length of the room before coming to a standstill right in front of Jack. Harrison was a good two feet taller, and a fair bit broader. The pose could be seen as threatening, but Jack saw what was on his face. He felt in no danger.

'I promise you, I had absolutely nothing at all to do with this. I didn't kidnap Freda and I haven't seen Desmond since that day at Nunhead cemetery a couple of months back.'

Jack was surprised to find he'd been holding his breath. He let it sigh out. 'OK. Well then, I don't know what's going on.'

'Can I see the crime scene?'

'No. I think you know that wouldn't be a good idea.'

It was Harrison's turn to sigh. He turned and walked back to the table. Jack could see his mind working overtime.

'How did they die?'

'Fire.'

'Fire?' Harrison raised his eyes to the ceiling and gave a knowing nod. 'So, how badly burnt are they?'

'Freda is partially burnt. Desmond was incinerated. Some kind of accelerant was used.'

'Then why do you think it's him?'

'His car was outside, and his jacket with ID was found in the house.'

Harrison snorted and shook his head.

'It's not him. Come on, Jack, you can see what he's done. You won't be able to properly identify that body, I bet. Freda's, yes. She was a dead woman, anyway. I told you they were plotting something, and this is it.'

'Why?'

'Why what?'

'Why go to all these lengths to stage your own murder. He could have spent the last few days of his life with Freda and then disappeared.'

'He's trying to make sure that nothing ever catches up with him, and I wouldn't be surprised if there wasn't something aimed at me in all this.'

'You sure you're not being paranoid?'

Harrison had sat back down in the chair and looked up at Jack from under his eyebrows.

'I'm sure,' he replied firmly.

There was a few moments' pause as both men thought.

'They think Freda died of a morphine overdose, not the fire.'

Harrison slammed his palm down onto the table.

'There you go, then. It was a mercy killing for her, so she didn't suffer. Believe you me, if I'd have killed her, I wouldn't have shown her mercy. She was killed by someone who cared about her.'

Jack took one look at Harrison's face and knew he was telling the truth. It was also the exact same thought that had gone through his head when he'd read Gordon's email earlier.

'Maybe that's the last we'll see or hear of Desmond then. You can at least get on with your life.'

Harrison gave a wry smile.

'Maybe, but I wouldn't be so sure.'

'The SIO, DI Gordon Jacobsen, he'll be thorough, which is good, but I've no doubt he'll be in touch with you. You were the last to visit Freda – officially – and he might discover you have motive.'

Harrison shrugged and nodded. 'There's nothing to tie me with the fire.'

'You got an alibi for early yesterday morning?'

'No. Tanya left about 1 a.m., and I was home alone until I left for work. CCTV at the flats?'

'I'll request that in case it gets deleted, so we've got it on system.'

A head bobbed into view above the frosted glass of the meeting room windows, distracting Jack, who peered out into the incident room.

He looked back at Harrison, who was sitting now with his hands on his lap, clearly thinking through the news he'd just heard.

'You OK if we start the briefing?' Jack asked him, aware that the team was beginning to gather outside. Last thing he wanted to do was draw attention to their conversation. Nothing worse than a room full of detectives when it came to gossip spreading.

Harrison nodded. Jack gave him one last scrutinising look before opening the door and beckoning the others in. Harrison looked defiant. There was no sign he was worried or scared. Jack wished he had his constitution. He wasn't sure he'd feel the same way in the circumstances.

THE TEAM TROOPED into the room, one by one. There were less of them today, and Jack could see instantly that he had a problem with morale. He needed to pull his focus off

Harrison and the Mannings, and get on with solving this case. He waited until everyone had sat down and the morning's greetings were over.

'I realise this isn't the most exciting case,' he began, feeling that a pep talk was required. 'We haven't got a body. There's no proof there's even been a murder, and, right now, all we have is a GBH assault charge, or possibly attempted murder, and a flu victim. But we still need to ensure justice is done. Themba Sisulu has been violently attacked. He might be a totally innocent bystander who has been injured through misidentification.

'And what about Anne Francis? Why did she die so quickly from a bout of flu? Could she have been murdered? Is there any truth to this curse, or is someone else behind her death? Just because we're not chasing around London knocking down doors and we don't have a confirmed murder victim in the morgue, doesn't make this case any less important. It has the potential to turn into a racial flashpoint, and we need to ensure that doesn't happen.'

Jack looked around the room at the faces, which, for the most part, were staring straight at him. DC David Oaks was as attentive and awake as always. Jack could rely on him – but the others? Detective Constable Geoff Richardson was positively comatose; Jack knew him and suspected he was close to burnout. There was a look that you came to recognise once you'd been in the force a while. It was in the eyes; a glazed, vacant stare that told of a brain which was overwhelmed and starting to go on strike.

Geoff had only recently finished on a particularly nasty child abuse case, so an elderly woman who died of flu, a bunch of paranoid Catholics, and an assault victim who it appears was going to be just fine, were complete trivia in comparison. Jack made a mental note to raise his concerns with Sandra. She was like a lioness when it came to her team and would throw a protective blanket around Geoff if she thought he was on the edge.

Sitting opposite Geoff was their youngest DC: Charlie, or Chaz Mitchell. His dad was a DCI up north somewhere, and Jack wasn't entirely sure whether Chaz had followed in his old man's footsteps out of choice, or under duress. Today he looked like he'd had one bevvy too many with the lads last night. His eyes were ringed red, and he kept having to stifle yawns.

Then there was Harrison's fan club, DC Rachel McGuire and Meera Kapadia. They were solid investigators, and the pair were trying to look attentive, but it was obvious that they were distracted by the object of their desire, Harrison. At least they looked more enthusiastic than the rest of them. Getting the team motivated was a hard sell.

'Right, let's have a quick review of where we are and see if we can't knock this one on the head.' Jack realised he was starting to sound like a primary school teacher. He briefly wondered if the suggestion of a quick game of tag outside in the car park might not wake them all up and get them going.

'Our inciting incident, outside the church. Are we any closer to identifying the two women or determining if the man was Themba?'

'Nothing more from Vice,' David spoke up.

'Yeah, not sure they're too worried about our little investigation, and I don't fancy being their whipping boy again.' Jack was concentrating so hard on keeping the momentum going that he completely missed his own faux pas. It did at least give Geoff something to smile at.

'How are we doing on CCTV from around the church on

the day of the alleged cursing?' Jack asked DC Mitchell, who'd been assigned the task of tracking down every available video footage of the area.

DC Charlie Mitchell woke his iPad up and scanned the screen. There was a moment of expectation as everyone looked to him. 'Not too productive.'

Jack sighed.

'I managed to locate around a dozen different cameras in the area, and once I'd discovered that two weren't actually working, we were left with ten. Unfortunately, the only one which covered the area that the incident took place is quite far away. I asked Josh in Video Imaging to work his magic, but even he can't get us anything better than this.'

Chaz's fingers skimmed across his iPad, he swiped, and the image appeared on the screen behind Jack. For a few moments, they all stared at a very grainy video of an African man with dreadlocks in a patterned shirt and what looked like jeans. Beside him were two African women in tight-fitting dresses and boots. Facing all three was a petite, white-haired woman. It was all in black and white and taken from what looked like the rooftop of a nearby property.

'I'd be barely able to recognise my own father from that, let alone a suspect,' Jack said. 'He could be Bob Marley for all we can see.'

'Actually, he couldn't,' Harrison interrupted from his seat. 'He's been dead since the 1980s.'

Jack gave him a stony stare. It would have been a lot more ferocious if it hadn't been for the fact he knew how much Harrison liked to stick to facts, and he wasn't being facetious.

'Yeah, I know it's not great,' DC Mitchell replied. 'But you can kind of see that he reaches into his pocket and then blows something in her face.'

All the police officers in the room subconsciously leant forward and squinted at the screen. It was true, you could just make out a light puff, and then Anne stepped back quickly and flapped at her face.

'Harrison, any thoughts? Could this be our killer curse?'

'It was certainly theatrics to give the effect of it being a curse, but in reality I suspect it was just some kind of ash or ground plant matter, and I don't see how it could be making other people ill.'

'So that's a no, then. We're just going round in circles with this. We can't say for sure if that man was or wasn't Themba. We have no idea what was blown into Anne's face. We still don't know why she died, other than medical experts saying it was flu.' Even Jack was getting frustrated.

'What about Themba? Hasn't he come out of the coma?' Harrison asked.

'He has, but he's refusing to talk. Just lies in bed staring at the ceiling. Won't eat, drink, or talk. They're getting a psychological assessment done.'

Jack paced back and forth around the room.

'Right, Rachel, you get over to Anne's house and see if you can find the clothes she was wearing on the day at church when our mystery man blew that stuff into her face. Be cautious, just in case it's some kind of hazardous substance. Make sure you're in full filter mask and suit.'

Rachel gave a thumbs up.

'Geoff, I need you to look into John Bellamy's and Stephen Chase's backgrounds. We've not dug that deeply, other than the obvious, because we had them in custody, but you never know. And, Harrison, can you go over to the hospital, see if you can work some of your own witch doctor magic and get Themba Sisulu talking to us?'

'Actually, there's one thing that's been bothering me,'

Harrison said frowning. 'Catholics believe in the resurrection. They're generally averse to being cremated, preferring instead to having their bodies buried on holy ground. Anne was devout; an old school Catholic. So why did Father Wilson get her cremated so quickly?'

18

Harrison didn't waste any time after the meeting. He was out of the incident room and on his bike before Jack could spring any more surprise information about the Mannings on him. He just didn't want to hear about them. Whatever was going to play out would play out. Jack may have had reservations, but Harrison knew Desmond wasn't dead. The game had begun – and it would include Harrison somewhere in the play.

He needed to focus on Themba right now. Harrison was convinced of the man's innocence, but was still perplexed as to why he had carried out a ritual on Anne's street the day John and Stephen attacked him.

Harrison arrived at the hospital just as a pale-faced father-to-be and his panting wife were arriving. She was clutching her huge stomach with one hand and holding on to his arm with the other. Harrison smiled at the scene. The man was wincing every few seconds because his partner's long nails were digging deep into his arm, but he obviously didn't dare complain due to the intense pain she was enduring to give birth to their child. The man was definitely in more of a panic than she was. It was a lovely scene to witness: the imminent arrival of new life, the celebration of two people about to become parents.

Harrison wasn't keen on hospitals usually. They always reminded him of when his grandmother died. She'd fought cancer, having operations and treatment after treatment, but although she'd won some battles, it had fought back and ultimately beaten her. He could still see her sitting in the hospital bed when he came to visit, always putting on a brave face and a smile, no matter how she felt.

It was the unique smells and sounds that took him back there. The slight mist in the air of antiseptic and anaesthetic. The bright white ceiling lights which hid nothing. The noise of the blood pressure machine, and the hushed rumble of a trolley bed being wheeled down a lino-floored corridor.

Harrison found the ward that Jack had told him to go to, but there was no sign of Themba. Most of the patients were dozing, letting sleep help them recover from whatever it was that had brought them into hospital. One man, with his entire leg in a cast, stared at him impassively as Harrison walked up and down, then returned his eyes to the small TV screen showing an episode of some daytime soap. Harrison wondered if the man could lip read because the volume was down so low.

Back in the main corridor, Harrison went in search of a nurse. He didn't need to go far. He found four of them huddled around a workstation. They were midway through a shift change briefing, but the arrival of a tall, dark, handsome man was a welcome respite.

'I'm looking for Themba Sisulu,' Harrison said to the four faces turned towards him. 'I'm with the Met Police.' He took his ID out and showed it to the nurses, who seemed to take an inordinately long time to carry out an examination of it and him.

'We've had to put him in his own room,' the woman who appeared to be the most senior, eventually said. 'He's still refusing to eat or drink. I'll show you.'

'Do you want me to take him, Clare, so you can get on with the handover?'

Clare looked at Harrison and then at her colleague, a young Filipino nurse, petite with neat bobbed hair and a beaming white smile.

'Go on then, Maj, thank you.'

Majallel Viola turned her smile up a further few degrees. 'This way.'

Behind Harrison, the rest of the nursing team allowed their eyes to linger on his receding back, before reluctantly returning their eyes to the paperwork.

'In here.' Maj smiled at Harrison and opened the door to a small private room. The curtains were open, but the TV wasn't on. Lying in the bed was Themba Sisulu, motionless, eyes open, staring at the ceiling.

'Mr Sisulu, my name is Dr Harrison Lane. I work with the Metropolitan police and we are trying to ensure that the people who hurt you are punished. Could you tell me what happened?'

Silence. There wasn't even a flicker or twitch on Themba's face. He lay like a sculptured effigy on a tomb. Not moving.

'He been like that since he woke up,' Maj explained. She walked over and checked on Themba's drip. 'Won't eat, won't drink. Won't talk. He getting worse.' She nodded to a rash that was forming on his face.

Harrison looked at him and then around the room.

'Where are his things?'

'Things?'

'Yes. What did he come in with? He should have had a stick and other bits with him.'

Maj thought a moment.

'No. Police took away. Came and bagged them up.'

Harrison pulled out his mobile phone and dialled Jack.

'Where are Themba Sisulu's belongings?' He barked his question to Jack the second he answered, not bothering with the usual niceties of phone conversations.

Jack was used to it.

'Probably taken as evidence.'

'He's a victim.'

'Yeah, but then the accusation that he'd cursed Anne came up and other people started falling ill, so I guess it was thought we should hang on to them just in case.'

'We need them back. He needs them back. If you don't, then he will die. He's not going to eat or drink and certainly isn't going to talk until you bring them here. I'm not sure anyone wants that on their conscience and in the papers.'

Maj was watching the one-way telephone conversation with interest. She was making herself busy checking on Themba's drip, but all the time, she studied Harrison from the corner of her eye.

'Thank you,' he said to her as he put his phone away. 'I'll stay until my colleague arrives.'

Maj realised he was dismissing her. She gave one last glance to her patient and one last, lingering look at Harrison, then slipped reluctantly out of the room.

'Themba, I understand you have been disconnected from your ancestors. I'm going to remedy that for you.' Harrison sat down in the chair across the other side of the room from the bed, watching the thin, motionless man. He wasn't sure, but he thought there was a flicker of something on Themba's face. Harrison waited for Jack. He had to come up with the goods.

Around ten minutes later, Harrison's mobile phone rang.

'Jack!' Harrison said to the phone as he answered it.

'What exactly are you after? I've got a few bags of stuff here, all seized from the crime scene or the hospital. I have to be careful here, Harrison. This is an ongoing case. I can't just take evidence away.'

'Tell me what you have.'

'There's a wooden stick with what looks like some kind of animal hair attached, and some beading.'

'We need that.'

'Various plant matter and an earthenware dish.'

'Nope.'

Harrison listened as Jack rummaged through the rest of the plastic bags in front of him.

'No idea what this is. Some kind of dried-up leathery thing with string or wool and more beads on it.'

'It's probably the gallbladder. We need that.'

'Whose gallbladder?'

'The goat that would have been sacrificed at Themba's initiation ceremony.'

'Eugh.'

More plastic rustling sounds.

'Then there's a blood-soaked cloth, looks like an African material.'

'Nope.'

'This looks like matches.'

'Nope.'

'A glass bottle. Whisky bottle. Empty.'

'Nope.'

'That's it then.'

'We need the stick and the gallbladder here, Jack, and what about the divination bones? Have they been tested yet?'

'I'll check, but I'm going to have to get permission. I'm not sure how long it will take.'

'I'll wait here for you to come. Tell them the longer they leave it, the worse Mr Sisulu's condition will become. He will die even if they try to keep him alive, because he will force his body to die. They won't be able to stop him.'

Harrison could have left the hospital rather than sit and wait it out, but in truth he was enjoying the quiet, and he also felt protective of the man whose room he sat in. In Themba's mind, he was powerless. Cut off from all he believed and in a strange country which had no concept of the world in which he belonged. He closed the door, shutting out the bustle of the ward, and sat back down in the chair.

While he waited, he caught up with some of his emails. There were the inevitable requests from various officers who were struggling to identify strange objects, or painted symbols found at crime scenes. He forwarded some of them on to Ryan, who was back in the office and champing at the bit for some mysteries to solve.

Harrison had already heard from Ryan several times that morning. He'd sent over the list of residents in Anne's street that Harrison had asked for. There was one which stood out to Harrison: a Robert Mbeki who, according to the census, lived in the street on his own. Harrison looked at the number and thought back to the road. It could be closer to where Themba was carrying out the ritual. Could Mr Mbeki be the target of his magic?

Harrison carried on working through his emails, answering as many as he could. Eventually, he reached his final unread message, sent late last night. It was an automated reply from the website where he'd recorded the theft of his motorbike helmet.

Harrison had just made a mental note to himself to swing by the bike shop after he'd finished at the hospital, when another thought entered his mind and sunk into his belly like a cold stone. Why had that lad targeted him? He already had a helmet. It wasn't valuable. At least, it wasn't valuable in itself. In the wrong hands, it might prove valuable to somebody. Somebody like Desmond Manning, who had planned to stage his own murder and that of his wife's. Was some of Harrison's DNA and hair about to be found at the crime scene in Putney?

19

It took Jack over an hour to persuade his bosses that it was not going to impact the case if he gave Themba his belongings back. He used the cultural significance argument to say they had to be returned. He didn't even pretend to understand the funny business that Harrison mentioned, but they couldn't ignore something which was important to their victim because of his race. That wouldn't look good in the diversity reports.

The first court hearing involving John Bellamy and Stephen Chase was after lunch, and they'd already submitted all their statements. No mention had been made by anyone of the stick being used to hit someone, and neither man had actually accused Themba of hitting them. Just to be sure, Jack took it via the Forensics lab for a quick fingerprint lift and swabs. There was always the possibility that John could have used the stick against Themba.

Mark Smith was one of the technicians on duty. He was a young guy, in his late twenties, who played in the police rugby team. Jack no longer played except for the odd match.

Once he'd made detective, the hours were more unpre-
dictable and when Marie had become pregnant, he decided
that the possibility of injuring himself when he needed to be
looking after his wife and newborn was too risky. Besides, it
was starting to hurt more. When he'd been younger, the
knocks had been more like bounces, now he felt every single
one and the recovery time was longer.

'You still playing?' Jack asked Mark as he focused on the
stick.

'Yeah, we're doing quite well this season and have a fair
few away matches. Beats sitting at home playing on the Xbox
every evening.'

Jack wished he had some spare evenings to do just that.

Jack knew that Mark had always wanted to be a forensics
investigator, ever since he'd first read Sherlock Holmes as a
child. Despite the high levels of awareness now, thanks to
countless TV crime dramas, Jack was grateful that criminals
still made mistakes. There was nothing more satisfying than
when Mark and his colleagues presented the investigating
team with a scrap of evidence that was sure to secure a
conviction.

'There are a couple of brown marks on the end here. I'll
just swab them to be sure they aren't blood stains,' Mark said.

Jack watched as Mark took some clean filter paper and
wiped over the stains, before adding some LMG – Leucoma-
lachite Green – followed by hydrogen peroxide. The filter
paper stayed a dirty-white colour. There was no blue-green
tinge to indicate that blood was present.

'Looks clean apart from those prints,' Mark finally said to
Jack, handing him back the stick.

'Cheers, mate,' Jack replied, looking at the stick in his
hands. How was this going to save a man from dying?

. . .

THE ANSWER to that question could be found sitting waiting for him in Themba Sisulu's hospital room. When Jack walked in, Harrison was sitting as motionless as the patient, his head bowed, eyes closed.

'Catching a nap? Tanya been keeping you up again?' Jack joked as he walked in. 'You'd better be right about this bloody stick and gallstone thing, had to put my neck on the line to persuade the guv to release them,' he continued.

'Gallbladder,' Harrison said, clicking out of the meditation he'd been in and immediately springing from the chair to meet him.

Jack crossed to the bed and looked at Themba. 'What's that rash on his skin? He looks worse.'

'He's ill because he has lost contact with his ancestral spirits. The gallbladder enables him to see beyond this world. In the initiation ceremony, they will have sacrificed the goat and then its gallbladder would have been hidden. He would have had to call on the ancestors to help him find where it was. The stick and the gallbladder were bestowed on him when he was initiated as a sangoma. Those white beads in his hair represent the connection with the spirits. He is a bridge between them and his people. He has a high status in his community at home.'

'And what do our doctors say about his condition? Could he have brain damage?'

'No. They can't find anything wrong.'

Jack pulled his lips together and frowned. He watched as Harrison took the stick from the bag first. It was a small animal whisk, no more than twenty inches long, with a brightly beaded handle and black hair flowing from the other end.

'What is that?' Jack asked, nodding at it.

'This was probably the tail of the ox that was sacrificed at Themba's initiation.'

'Not great to be a farm animal then when it comes to an initiation ceremony,' Jack snarked.

'They would have been eaten by the village at a feast,' Harrison replied.

He gently lifted one of Themba's hands, which lay across his torso, placed the stick on the man's chest and then his hand back on top so that he could feel it. Next, Harrison took the dried leathery gallbladder from its bag.

'This should be tied into his hair at the back, but I assume the doctors or nurses took it off when he came in.'

Harrison repeated the process, this time lifting his other hand and placing the gallbladder onto Themba's chest, replacing his hand on top.

Finally, he took the small bag of divination bones and placed them close to his fingertips.

Jack looked at Themba and then up at Harrison.

'What now?'

'We give him a moment to reconnect.'

Jack looked back at Themba and noticed that he had closed his eyes. They were no longer staring at the ceiling.

'I'm going to go and get a coffee then. You want something?'

'A bottle of water, please.'

'Do you think this will take long?' Jack asked, nodding at Themba.

'Difficult to say, you can't rush these things.'

Jack muttered under his breath and left.

HARRISON SAT BACK DOWN to watch Themba. He had started moving his fingers, gently stroking and touching the precious items that Harrison had placed on his chest. Behind his eyelids, Harrison could see his eyes flickering and moving. He was going into a dream state, reconnecting with his spirits.

By the time Jack had returned with his paper cup of coffee and Harrison's water, Themba was whispering and murmuring under his breath. His lips barely moved, but he was saying something.

'Progress, that's good,' Jack said to Harrison, sitting himself in the only other remaining chair in the room.

A few minutes passed, Jack finished his coffee and got up to put the cup in the bin. On his way back to the chair, he peered at Themba.

'How much longer?' Jack asked Harrison. Jack was about to walk away when Themba's eyes suddenly shot open and he said something in his native tongue.

'Shit!' Jack jumped back, shocked by the sudden movement.

When he looked at Harrison, he was smiling.

'Yeah, hilarious.' Jack turned to Themba. 'Mr Sisulu, we're from the Metropolitan Police. We're hoping to talk to you about what happened – about why you were attacked.'

Themba slowly turned and looked at Jack. His voice was dry and cracked and he struggled to talk above a whisper. 'Bones must be thrown in three places before the message can be accepted.'

Jack's mouth dropped open, and he looked at Harrison, eyebrows raised.

Harrison stood up and came over to the bed. 'I believe that what he means is you need to consider that question in several different ways before you will find the answer or reach a decision. It's relating to a divination ritual when he speaks to his ancestors.'

Jack decided to try a slightly different tack. 'Mr Sisulu, would you like to sit up and have a drink?'

Themba nodded.

'I'll get a nurse in. She can make you more comfortable; I don't want to disturb the drip.'

Jack quickly left the room and went in search of a nurse.

Themba turned to Harrison. 'Thank you for bringing me back to my ancestors,' he said. 'In London there are no mountains to lift me closer to speak to my spirits, and without these,' he pointed to his stick, the gallbladder, and bones, 'I am silenced.'

Harrison nodded an acknowledgement. 'Why have you come here?'

'I answered a call to heal, but when I arrived, the spirits said the community is broken. They tell me you will help.'

The door opened, interrupting Themba, and a nurse marched in, closely followed by Jack. She was below average in height, but what she lacked in feet, she made up for with character.

'Mr Sisulu, it's good to see you with us,' she said in a broad Irish accent that meant business. 'Gentlemen, why don't you step outside a moment and give Mr Sisulu some privacy while I get him more comfortable.'

Jack and Harrison quickly left the room.

'Did he say anything while I was out?' Jack asked Harrison in a hushed tone.

'He said *Thank you*, and I asked him why he was here. He said it was to heal.'

'To heal?'

'He's a healer – that's what he does, so stands to reason.'

'Heal who?'

'Didn't get that far, but he said the community is broken.'

'Well, he got that right. He's not going to talk in riddles and African proverbs all the time, is he?'

Harrison shrugged and smiled.

Jack's mobile rang in his pocket.

'DS Salter. Yup. Shit. Who? How many? OK.'

Harrison watched on quizzically. Whatever it was, it didn't look like good news.

'I've got to go. A Facebook group has sprung up making wild claims about Anne being murdered by African black magic and John Bellamy and Stephen Chase being innocent. It's stirring up racial tensions. There are already people gathering outside the courtroom. The Territorial Support Group are on their way now. This is just what we'd hoped to avoid.

'You talk to Themba, find out what he's doing here, who he's involved with. We'll need to take a proper statement from him, so get him prepped for that. I'll send David as soon as I can.'

Harrison watched Jack's back hurrying off down the corridor just as the door to Themba's room re-opened and the nurse popped her head out.

'He's all ready for you now.'

20

A large crowd had gathered inside the tall green security fencing that surrounded Woolwich Crown Court. Within the hour, Stephen Chase and John Bellamy's bail hearing would take place in one of the high-security courtrooms. Protestors carried placards with Stephen's and John's faces and slogans including *Free our brothers*; *God is the Judge*; and *Justice for Anne*, while singing hymns and lighting candles.

They were being watched by a row of Territorial Support Group police officers, dressed in black with high-vis green bibs marked with the clear identification of POLICE. There was nobody from the firearms squad present, but Jack knew the TSG guys would have a van nearby with riot gear should the situation turn ugly. The court security guards and a handful of regular uniformed police bolstered their numbers.

When Jack arrived, the scene was calm, but news camera crews and newspaper reporters had got wind and were circling, asking for interviews and digging into the rotten underbelly of the story. Tabloid reporters were gorging on the lurid claims of black magic and witchcraft.

He heard one interviewee – somebody they'd not spoken to in their inquiry – passionately talking to a reporter. 'She was an innocent churchgoing woman trying to help victims of trafficking. This is an attack on British society. More people are falling sick and the authorities are trying to send the wrong men to prison.'

Jack could feel his heart rate racing. This had the potential to turn into something very ugly. They had to get to the bottom of what happened to Anne and identify the man who was outside the church that day. If it wasn't Themba, who was it? He spotted the red, white, and black logo of Sky News and realised the team was about to go live. Jack pulled out his phone to call DCI Sandra Barker and warn her there could be a backlash.

Jack was on his mobile when he saw Father Wilson arrive. The rector walked into the area outside the court and was immediately embraced by people. He disappeared into the middle of the crowd, still smiling, but looking a little overwhelmed by it all. Jack watched him being carried along by the sea of people. Some Father Wilson clearly recognised, others he appeared to be meeting for the first time. He was being treated like a hero.

'There's already been some graffiti sprayed at the church,' DCI Barker was telling Jack. 'If Themba Sisulu is now talking, we need to confirm if he's got an alibi for the day of the cursing, and, if he has, that has to be released to the media ASAP. The last thing we need is him being targeted again. Are we any closer to getting some answers, Jack?'

'We're working on it,' was all he could say. He was acutely aware that something like this could suddenly blow up. All it would take was a tiny spark, and the tinderbox of ignorant prejudices would be set alight.

Jack searched in the crowd again for Father Wilson, but couldn't see him. Perhaps he'd gone inside. John and Stephen were due in court in ten minutes. They would have made their way from Belmarsh prison, along the tunnel that led between it and the courts. It was a secure way of transporting prisoners between the two, and thankfully meant there were no emotional scenes as prisoners arrived outside the court in a van.

Jack looked for the Territorial Support commander and spotted a face he recognised. Sergeant Matt Dean had been at Lewisham before being recommended for TSG about a year ago.

Jack remembered one infamous day at the station when Matt had challenged another officer, whose nickname was Meat Loaf, to an arm wrestle in the canteen. PC Brown, aka Meat Loaf, bore more than a passing resemblance to the singer, but was taller and fitter, and there were few in the force, or on the streets, who would dare to challenge him. Matt was about half his width, but incredibly fit and, most importantly, had the temperament of a Jack Russell terrier. Matt thought himself bigger than he was, wasn't afraid to take on anything, and didn't give up.

The ensuing arm wrestle went on for so long that officers were pulled away from their desks to come and watch. A huge, testosterone-filled crowd had gathered around the pair like some ancient Roman gladiatorial battle, cheering and encouraging them on. In the end it had been the sheer stubbornness of the Jack Russell which had beaten the sheer bulk of the bear.

Matt won just in the nick of time because the head chef, tired of all the noise and disruption in her canteen, had decided enough was enough. The spectre of the larger-than-life, angry, red-faced woman marching out brandishing a large wooden spoon, sent the pack of grown men running for safety like naughty toddlers. In the meantime, Matt went down in station history as being a tough nut and, soon after, he'd transferred to TSG.

'Matt, how's it going?' Jack said as he came up alongside him.

'Salty, mate, good to see you. So far all quiet, but I've had word that there's some intel coming in on people calling for retaliation. It's polarising sections of the community and the usual suspects are jumping on the bandwagon.'

'Do you think they'll turn up here?'

'Gut feeling. I don't reckon so. This lot are watered-down radicals. The ones we're worried about – the ones who are spreading the tension – it's too public for them. We're talking far right individuals who like to stir the shit but not end up on the front page of a tabloid themselves. School teachers, investment bankers, and even civil servants. What we're more likely to see is their propaganda turning this into a shit wagon that attracts the flies who want to cause trouble.'

Jack sighed. They had to get on top of this before people got hurt.

21

At the hospital, Harrison had been allowed back into Themba's room, and was sitting next to his bed watching him tuck into a plate of hospital beef casserole. Harrison had moved closer to him because his voice was still weak and he hadn't wanted him to strain his throat.

Harrison noticed that Themba had replaced the gall-bladder in his hair and was already beginning to look better than even just an hour ago. The power of the mind to heal the body, or destroy it, never ceased to amaze him.

He'd already found out that Themba was over in the UK to visit a friend who was sick. The only problem was, Themba wouldn't say who the friend was for fear of getting them into trouble.

'You're here legally – there's no need to protect them, and you need to tell us because, otherwise, you have no one to give you an alibi,' Harrison explained to him now.

Themba shook his head. 'The harmful fly sent by a wicked man can do no harm.'

Harrison sighed and was glad that Jack wasn't still with them. The conversation would have frustrated him. 'Can you tell me what happened the day of the attack?'

'The two men jumped out of a car. I had no reason to fear them, but one of them came over and stamped out the fire I had made to burn offerings. He was shouting. I know men like him. He did not like my skin. He used words against me. Bad words which would get him into trouble back home.'

'He was being racist?'

'Yes. And he called me a witch doctor and juju priest. That made me angry. He was trying to claim that I was a bad man.'

'He is prejudiced and ignorant,' Harrison replied. 'He will be punished for what he did to you, but we also need to prove that you aren't the man he talked about. The man who he says put a curse on his church and friend.'

'I came to heal sickness,' Themba said. 'In my dreams, I see the cavern that opens. You understand that sickness is not like they treat it here.' Themba waved his arms around the room. 'Sickness comes from the spirit and society. The natural order has been disturbed in your community and people will continue to be sick until that is treated.'

Harrison tried to read between the lines of what Themba was saying and suspected it might have more to do with Stephen Bellamy and John Chase than the reason why Themba had originally come over.

Harrison nodded at him, and was surprised to find Themba's hand suddenly clasping his arm. Then Themba lent forward and earnestly looked into his face.

'Look to the coloured squares,' he said. 'The spirits tell me they hold the answers.' He held Harrison's gaze for a few more seconds and then let his hand and arm slip back down as he relaxed once more.

Harrison now had absolutely no idea what Themba was referring to, and the arrival of DC David Oaks, just a minute or so later, was a welcome break from the intensity of trying to communicate with someone who saw the world from a completely different perspective to himself. Despite all his years of reading and research, he could only come so far in his understanding of Themba's culture and beliefs. All Harrison could do was respect them. One thing he did know for sure though was that Themba wasn't the man at the church.

DC David Oaks arrived on a waft of aftershave which helped sweeten the hospital air, and his positive attitude was exactly what was needed. Harrison told the young detective all that he'd gleaned so far and then left Themba in DC Oaks' capable hands so he could take an official statement.

HARRISON HAD A HUNCH. That list of residents on Anne's road had a Robert Mbeki down as living in house number 66. If he could at least verify Themba's alibi, then they could concentrate their efforts on finding the mystery pimp who was alleged to have cursed Anne and the church and made them sick. The investigation was being complicated unnecessarily. In his mind, these were two totally separate incidents – and confirming that would help them all see clearer.

Harrison rode over to Anne's and followed the house numbers up the road. As he'd suspected, Mr Mbeki's house was opposite the area that Themba had been attacked. It was all making sense now.

Number 66 had been newly decorated and looked as though its owner had plenty of money to maintain it. The front garden was neat and manicured, with the borders full of what Harrison guessed to be African daisies. There were no flowers left at this time of year, but he could imagine the whole garden packed with their colourful faces in warmer weather.

Harrison rang the doorbell and waited. The gloss black paint of the door reflected the pale winter sun, and he could see himself, a fuzzy grey shadow, on its surface. There was no answer, and so he rang again, pressing the brass button and listening to the shrill ring inside the hallway. Still no answer. Harrison was just backing away from the door and giving up when he heard the locks on the inside being opened and the door slowly swung open.

An overweight black man in his sixties stood in front of Harrison, leaning on a stick and obviously in pain.

'Mr Mbeki?'

'Yes.'

'I'm Dr Harrison Lane. I'm with the Ritualistic Behavioural Crime unit at the Metropolitan Police, and I'm working with my colleagues on piecing together why a man called Themba Sisulu was attacked here a week or so ago. I understand you might know him?'

Mr Mbeki frowned. 'You had better come in.'

HARRISON STEPPED inside a beautifully kept hallway. This was not somewhere that you walked in with muddy boots. Robert Mbeki nodded towards an open doorway and Harrison went through into a sitting room of cream leather and rugs, interspersed with brightly coloured African ornaments and animal skins. It was a lovely room with windows at both ends, and clearly one Mr Mbeki spent a great deal of time in. A large leather chair was centre stage, surrounded by books and paperwork, like a giant human nest. It was to there that Robert slowly hobbled.

'I cannot offer you tea, I am afraid. As you can see, I am not too mobile these days and the housekeeper is out. She will be back in about half an hour. You are welcome to have one then.'

'Not to worry, I'm fine.' Harrison reassured him.

Mr Mbeki positioned the back of his calf muscles against the large chair facing Harrison. He took tiny shuffling steps to get in place. Then he virtually collapsed down into the chair with a half groan and half sigh, attempting to slow his descent by using his arms to support himself.

'Rheumatoid arthritis, the doctors here tell me,' he said to Harrison. 'But you have not come about me. How is Themba?'

'He's recovering well now. I suspect he'll be discharged in the next forty-eight hours. They just need to make sure he's eating and drinking and strong enough.'

'Good. I heard them call him a witch doctor, said something about him putting a curse on a woman. These are all lies.'

'I believe it's a case of mistaken identity, Mr Mbeki, but I have some questions.'

Robert Mbeki nodded, but then winced and shifted in his seat.

'Can I get you something?' Harrison asked. It was obvious he was in a great deal of pain.

'No. I am afraid this is debilitating when it flares up. I had been feeling better, but when Themba was attacked, I lost his prayers and his muti.'

'Can I see the muti that Themba gives you?'

Mr Mbeki studied Harrison.

'I know what some people think, Dr Lane, but he is not here to sacrifice babies or even adults. I saw the story in the papers and the reporters mentioned the boy's torso found in the Thames years ago. The priests behind muti killings and those who practise human sacrifice, they have black hearts. I see what you have on your mind and it is not that.'

'I understand. I don't think Themba is a bad man either, but we have to prove that he's not a danger, and to do that we must counter the prejudice of John Bellamy and Stephen Chase. I have to show what it is that Themba does do.'

'Very well. I have some snuff for the headaches I get from the pain, and I have a drink which is to reduce the inflammation. I am nearly all out of them, but I will allow you to take a small sample, to prove Themba's innocence.'

'You paid for Themba to come over here to help you?'

'Yes. He is from my home village. I have been gone a long time, but I still hold my culture in my heart, Dr Lane. He is a healer, not a witch doctor. I arranged for the ingredients to make his medicines to be brought over for him. I am a wealthy man, but money is no good to me if it does not make my health better. I suppose you think I am foolish? I do trust in the expertise of your British doctors, but our way is the natural way, Dr Lane. There is also only so much your medicines can do.

'I believe that illness is much more than just a physical cause. It is spiritual and cultural. Themba consults with our ancestral spirits, and they can see the imbalance within me, and show him how to help me. I know my people are with me, even when I am not in my homeland, and that gives me something more powerful than just drugs. It gives me hope.'

'I understand, Mr Mbeki. I'm not here to judge you.'

Robert gave Harrison a small nod of acknowledgement and lent down to the cupboard beside his chair. He took out a dark-green powder in a small plastic Ziploc bag.

Harrison got up and walked over to him, taking an evidence bag out of the pocket in his jacket.

Mr Mbeki sighed, clearly a little taken aback by its formality, but he sprinkled some of the green powder into the bag. Then he pulled out a bottle. It was virtually empty.

'You can take this. I have one more full one.'

'Thank you.' Harrison held open another bag and Robert placed it inside, watching Harrison seal it afterwards.

'How often was Themba coming to see you?'

'Every day.'

'So was he with you two weeks ago on Tuesday?'

'He had not missed a day since he arrived, not until the attack.'

'What time does he come?'

'11:30 a.m. until about 2 p.m. He is not working, you understand? I am not paying him. He is a friend. I merely paid for his trip over to visit me. We are not doing anything illegal and his visa runs out in less than three months. Then he will return home.' Robert had suddenly become more animated as he realised he could be getting himself and Themba into trouble.

'It's fine. We're not trying to cause you or Themba any further difficulties. We're aware he's here on a visa for six months, and if he wants to visit you each day, then that's his prerogative.'

'Thank you. I may end up going back with him. Get away from the British winter and find some warmth in my homeland. It is just hard with my business interests, that is all.'

'Could I ask you what business you do, Mr Mbeki?'

'Sure, sure. I import African hair and make-up products. I also supply many European countries too. Brexit has been a paperwork nightmare, I can tell you.'

'Is there anyone else who could verify that Themba was here with you that Tuesday?'

'My housekeeper, Mary. She would have seen him. She

buys the fruit and vegetables he needs, so they meet every day.'

'Thank you. One of my colleagues will make an appointment to get a formal statement from yourself and your housekeeper either this afternoon or tomorrow.'

Robert Mbeki nodded.

'I can let myself out.'

Mr Mbeki raised his hand by way of a goodbye and thank you. Harrison saw him lean back in his chair and close his eyes. The pain clearly ruled his life and Harrison could understand why he was willing to try anything. Was he willing to use black magic? Black magic that could kill?

As Harrison got back on his Harley, he ran through the many different possibilities. Could Robert Mbeki be involved in a people-smuggling ring? Or had he lied about Themba's muti? Would he think that some kind of sacrifice of people to harness their spirits could make him better? Gut instinct told Harrison no, and he suspected that the muti, or medicine, that he had in the evidence bag, combined with what they'd found at Themba's flat, would prove his innocence.

Harrison was about to head straight to Lewisham and the forensics lab when a thought crossed his mind. Themba's flat was only a few streets away. Themba probably walked the same route every day to Robert Mbeki's – and that might take him past a CCTV camera. Harrison checked Google Maps. There was only one way that Themba could realistically walk. Harrison started his bike and set off to follow it.

Most of the route was via residential streets. It was possible that somebody had a doorbell camera, or security cameras, but the main road was Harrison's most likely bet. He wasn't disappointed. A small supermarket, hairdresser and a pizza takeaway all displayed cameras. He took a photograph on his phone and sent it to Ryan. He hoped that this might mean they could close down that line of enquiry.

Looking at the shops reminded Harrison that he still needed to get his new helmet. The motorbike shop was on the way back to Lewisham. He could swing by there quickly and replace his stolen one.

IT WASN'T A BIG RETAILER, but they managed to pack in a great deal of stock and it was one of the most popular stockists among hardcore bikers. The front of *The Best Gear* was a little tired, but the windows were always full of brand names and the latest helmet or leathers. It sat, rather incongruously, between a kebab shop which had named itself, *The Best Kebab*, and a garish pink-painted nail bar, *Posh n Polish*.

The motorbike accessories shop was a regular haunt for Harrison – it was where he got most of his kit from – but he'd never tried its neighbouring establishments. The other side of the street was a bike showroom, also owned by the same two brothers. Harrison hadn't bought his bike from there, but he'd often wandered around looking at the eye candy.

Harrison scanned the racks of helmets in *The Best Gear*. They didn't seem to have exactly the same design he'd lost, although there was one which was similar. He asked anyway, just in case they had one in the stockroom.

'That one's discontinued now,' one of the brothers said. He was the most tattooed of the pair, and nearly as broad as he was tall. His brother was slimmer, with short hair and sideburns that gave him the look of Peter Fonda in *Easy Rider*. This brother was more ZZ Top than Dennis Hopper. He scratched at his long brown beard. 'Getting lots of interest today for that one. Had a copper in here earlier asking about it. Seems they found one at a crime scene.'

Harrison showed nothing on his face, not even a glimmer of interest or shock, but his stomach knotted. It had to be his, but which crime scene? Was it in the house where the fire had been, or somewhere else? Or was he being totally paranoid, and it had been a snatch-and-grab raid by youths after all, and the helmet was now in the middle of some jewellery shop break-in investigation? He suspected he would soon be finding out.

The shop owner was studying his face. Harrison knew he recognised him. He was one of those men who could remember what he'd sold and to whom, usually offering up suggestions of things Harrison might like based on his past purchasing. A kind of human Amazon algorithm.

Harrison knew full well that going back to buy the same helmet a couple of days after one had been left at a crime scene looked suspicious. But he also knew the guy was tipping him off, not planning on ratting on him. There was a code among bikers.

As Harrison walked out of the shop, his mobile rang. Jack.

'Where are you? We need you back here ASAP. There have been some developments and David's on his way back with Themba's statement.' Jack sounded harassed, almost curt with him, which was out of character. The stress was clearly getting to him.

'I was just getting a new helmet. I'm done. Be with you in twenty minutes,' he replied and jumped on his bike.

22

Jack ended the call to Harrison and looked at his incident board. This morning it had been mostly bare space, but now he'd returned to Lewisham police station to find the team had sprung to life and there were new names on the board, and new potential motives. DCI Barker was also on his back. What had initially seemed to be an assault case was now looking more like murder and at last it had piqued the interest of his team. You could almost smell the increase in adrenaline in the air.

Harrison and DC David Oaks both arrived at the station at the same time, Harrison pulling into the car park just after DC Oaks.

'I think I've sorted his alibi,' Harrison said after he'd walked over to meet the detective.

'Really? He refused to give me a name,' DC Oaks said, surprised.

'He didn't need to. The house opposite where he was attacked is owned by a South African businessman. He brought Themba over.' They were walking up the stairs now towards the incident room, and Harrison had to pause his explanation as David acknowledged another colleague. 'He paid for him to come over and heal his arthritis,' he continued. 'We might have CCTV proof as well as his sponsor's say so.'

'Well, Themba was adamant anyway that it wasn't him at the church, so we're back to square one,' DC Oaks said dejectedly as he pushed open the incident room door.

The minute Jack saw them both, he shouted to the team, 'Briefing room now for an update.'

Everyone finished typing the sentence they were on, or ended the phone call they were having, and filed back into the briefing room. There was a noticeable fizz in the room which hadn't been there that morning.

'Right, everyone.' Jack didn't wait for them to sit down. He started immediately. 'We have got a potentially highly flammable situation on our hands right now. This case has just got bigger, and it's blown our original hypotheses out the window. Geoff.'

Jack nodded to DC Richardson to take the floor.

'Facebook posts started appearing, claiming that Anne was murdered by African black magic and that John Bellamy and Stephen Chase are innocent. In fact, they're heroes protecting our Catholic community here in London which is under attack, don't you know.

'In some of them, the language was fruity and encouraging violence. Other posts were more subtle, appealing more to the middle-class armchair racist. Facebook has pulled them down, but you can be sure they're circulating on other, less public, channels. We've traced those posts back to known British National Party supporters and far-right activists.

'Turns out that John Bellamy has links to some of these

men. We're continuing to research his connections to see how deeply he's involved, but, needless to say, our holier-than-thou Mr Bellamy is not such a saintly individual after all.

'The vitriol is obviously stirring up racial tensions and the Catholic Church has been targeted with graffiti. It's not going to take much for us to see some serious consequences.'

Jack interrupted. 'We've also just heard that, as we suspected, John and Stephen got bail. Not sure where the money to pay that bail order has come from because it's not an insignificant amount.' He raised his eyebrows at the team and nodded back to DC Geoff Richardson, who continued.

'John Bellamy is the church treasurer. He's been running an active campaign to fundraise for the repairs needed to shore up a wall of the building. They seem to have all been pretty active in this regard, but are still a couple of hundred thousand away from their target. They're not cosmetic repairs. If they don't stabilise the wall, it could be catastrophic for the church.'

'Do you think it's all a publicity ploy to get sympathy donations?' DC David Oaks asked.

'Maybe one motive, but something far more interesting has come up.' DC Richardson paused a moment, looking at his audience for effect. 'Anne had signed over everything in her will to the church. Her house alone is worth around three quarters of a million pounds and we're already uncovering several other savings accounts that she'd accrued over the years.'

Geoff paused again to let that sink in. 'Dr Lane, it throws further weight and importance on your question as to why Anne was cremated. It all seems incredibly convenient that John Bellamy gets to further his own racist agenda, as well as save the church at the same time. Plus, we know there wasn't an autopsy. Anne's own doctor pronounced her dead and wrote it down as complications from the flu that had led to pneumonia and heart failure. If somebody had smothered her somehow, then we aren't ever going to know.'

There was silence in the briefing room as the whole team thought through what DC Richardson had just suggested.

'What about Father Wilson? Do you think he's in on it?' DC Oaks asked.

'I'm not sure, but it was his decision to cremate Anne,' Geoff replied.

'So are you thinking that the juju priest had nothing to do with Anne's death? That we've been totally focused on the wrong incident?' DC Rachel McGuire spoke now.

'Not necessarily. Whatever it was that he blew onto Anne could have made her ill. What I'm concerned about is how quickly she seemed to die and then have her body disposed of. So perhaps what's more likely is that somebody saw an opportunity, a scapegoat, and grabbed it.'

'Her clothes are with Forensics. They might be able to give us some preliminary results on any residues they've found by now,' Rachel added.

'Get on to them,' Jack said to her.

Rachel quickly typed an email on her phone.

'I also want to know the exact movements of John Bellamy and Stephen Chase for that period between the so-called cursing and Anne's death. Did anyone else see her alive after John and Stephen visited the day they attacked Themba?

'Get Forensics into Anne's house. Geoff: go through John's, Stephen's and the church's finances with a fine-tooth comb. Call in Financial Crime expertise if you think it's warranted. This case is already hitting the national headlines and we are coming under increasing pressure to get this sorted before we have wide-scale violence to deal with.' Jack paused a moment and looked at Harrison. 'Anything you want to add, Dr Lane?'

'We can finalise one element of our enquiries. Themba Sisulu has an alibi for the day of the cursing: the man who sponsored him to come over, and his housekeeper. Themba wasn't the man at the church. It was an unprovoked attack on him, whether through mistaken identity or some other motive, but he is an innocent victim in this. We should get that out to the press so he isn't targeted.'

'And we're sure they're not lying for him?'

'I think we'll be able to get CCTV evidence to back it up. I've said all along that I thought it was mistaken identity. Themba wasn't there in connection with Anne. He was there for Robert Mbeki, who lives at number 66. That's opposite where the attack took place. Anne lived at number 33. It never made sense that he was so far down the road.'

'OK, so are we any closer to finding out who our mystery juju priest was?'

The room shook their heads.

'Sir,' DC Rachel McGuire interrupted, 'I've just had a reply back. The lab thinks the powders on Anne's clothes are just harmless ash. They are going to run a few more tests, but so far they can't find any toxins or pathogens that could make anybody ill.'

'Then we can forget worrying about our juju priest. Good, the field is narrowing.'

'I'm sceptical that John Bellamy would have hurt Anne,' Harrison spoke again. 'I think he loved her.'

The team turned to look at Harrison as they took in that latest statement.

'So, he's covering up an affair? That's motive enough for a married Catholic man.' Geoff frowned.

Harrison shook his head. 'Not in that way – I think Anne

was totally devoted to her God and only him. Did you notice there were no mirrors in her home? No images of herself. Her clothes were very plain and while her home was comfortable, there were no luxuries. She was as close to being a nun as possible, without the habit.'

'You really think John fancied her then?'

'I think he loved her piety and virtues. She was a white Catholic, almost certainly a virgin who had lived her life for the church and its community. Those values seem to represent everything he thinks he's standing for. All that is white and good in his warped racist mind. It's not so much a lustful love as loving admiration.'

'So you're saying you don't think she was murdered?' Geoff asked Harrison now, with a challenging tone to his question.

Harrison chose his words carefully. 'I'm saying if she was murdered – and I don't know if she was or not – I don't think it was John. We need to keep an open mind about this. We're dealing with incredibly deeply rooted beliefs, from the African black magic curse, the Catholic faith, and the white supremacists. Add money into that pot and that's when you'll get people behaving very out of character.'

'OK, enough debate. We need to get on with investigating this case and getting to the bottom of what happened,' Jack interrupted. 'Harrison is right, we do need to keep an open mind, but let's start by rattling John Bellamy's cage and see what falls out. I want all resources focused on him and the others at the church. That congregation is set to benefit by what we think could be close to a million pounds, thanks to Anne's death. It's more than enough of a motive.'

The briefing room door opened, causing most of the team to lift their heads to see who was coming in late. It was the boss, DCI Sandra Barker.

'Father Wilson has just been on the phone, tells me there's now over half a dozen people who aren't well and many of them are very elderly, so not strong. He is going to hold a special service tonight in the church to cleanse it of the curse.'

'OK, thanks boss. So, following our discussion, I want as many of you there as possible to keep a close eye on what's going on. We need to be all over that church and its congregation.'

'Will John and Stephen go?' Geoff asked.

'I'm not sure. Father Wilson said he doesn't want them fanning any unrest in the community, so they might stay away. However, he said he wouldn't turn them away if they came,' DCI Barker replied.

'John will go,' Harrison said. 'Maybe not Stephen, but John will see it as his right and he won't be stopped by anyone.'

'Maybe you've got a good point there, Harrison,' Jack added. 'Stephen could be our weak link. Perhaps we should pay him another visit – without being accused of harassment. I'm sure we could find some new evidence or lines of enquiry that we need to put to him.'

23

Patience pocketed the man's money and left him to gather himself before he resumed his life. He was one of what she called the *shadow men*, who in the daylight lived a respectable family existence, with a wife and children – a good job too, by his clothes. But when the shadows fell, he would seek her out for something he wasn't getting at home. Sometimes it was because the wife was no longer interested in his needs. She often heard the sob stories and excuses of cold shoulders and empty beds. Most often she could empathise with the wife, the woman whose name he would speak, as she serviced him for her. Other times they came to her because they needed something different. A little bit of African spice. She had her limits, but *different* often meant more money, so it was tempting.

In all honesty, she didn't care about their lives in the sunlight. It was how they were to her in the shadows that mattered. If they were polite or businesslike, then that was a good job. Some talked a lot. Others barely said a word. All that mattered to her was moving on to the next client.

This man had been quick and polite. He smelled of soap and aftershave. His breath wasn't rancid with beer and his hands gentle. She decided it was a good way to end her day. In other weeks, she might have stayed to score another turn until Florence arrived. They worked the same patch, alternating the day and night shifts. Sometimes the men didn't even notice the difference. Since Florence's beating, Patience had been working alone, putting in extra hours to help her friend with her payments to Madam. There were never good enough excuses not to pay her.

Today she wanted to get back to the flat. Florence hadn't looked well this morning. She was hot and feverish, and Patience was worried.

On the way back, she bought some milk and eggs. If she cooked Florence something soft, maybe she would eat it. Since the attack, she'd not really touched any food. Lately she'd talked about dying, about wanting to die.

As Patience put the key in the lock, she felt a sense of foreboding. What if Florence died, or was already dead? She pushed open the grubby, cracked door and walked into the dark flat, calling out to her. There was no reply.

Immediately, she put down the shopping and opened her friend's bedroom door. The light from the hallway shafted in and fell across the mattress on the floor that Florence slept on. She was uncovered and her body was gleaming with sweat, and yet Patience could see her shivering. Little shudders ran all through her body, making her skin shimmer in the light. Her breathing was rapid and shallow, rippling her solar plexus muscle but barely lifting her chest. Patience put her hand to her mouth and nose. The smell had got worse. She'd cleared up the vomit, but this was different. It smelt like rotting flesh.

Patience called Florence's name and went to her, putting her hand on her forehead. It was burning. Her friend struggled to open her eyes and looked up at her.

'Mama,' she said in their native Nigerian tongue. She reached out for Patience; a hot, clammy hand. She was hallucinating.

Patience reassured her, talking gently. She didn't try to correct her. It was better that she believed she was home with her mother at her side, than here in the dark, injured and sick. Patience went into the kitchen and rinsed through the scrap of towel she had used to cool Florence's forehead. Then she sat with her friend, alternately holding her hand and trying to get her to sip some water, but the water mostly just dribbled from her lips.

Patience realised that Florence was dying. An infection had taken hold of her body and now her mind. Before long it would take her soul. Her own tears fell for her friend; big, fat tears that splashed off her chin and onto her legs. She began to rock back and forth. What should she do? They needed help, but from where? She had just one telephone number: their madam, the woman who had sponsored their trip. She was allowed to call nobody but her.

Almost an hour later, she heard the sound of a key going into the lock on the front door. There was a chain across it and so Patience got up from the floor beside Florence. Her legs were stiff from the kneeling, and tension from the worry had made her muscles all through her body hurt.

'Who is it?' she called out to the person in Nigerian.

'Madam,' was the one-word reply. She had no other name to them.

Patience unlatched the chain and let Madam in.

'What is that stench?' she asked her, scowling. Madam

was from Nigeria, but had lived in the UK for almost twenty years. She wore bright-pink lipstick and had green eyeshadow on with perfectly coiffured hair and painted red nails.

Patience wanted to be like Madam. Her clothes were always clean and expensive-looking. She didn't need to show her body to make her money and so they were fitted but discreet. She was a businesswoman, and today, she was angry. It made Patience feel ashamed.

Madam pulled a tissue from her pocket and held it over her nose and mouth. Then she peered into the room at Florence.

She swore. 'Why she in such a state?'

'She was attacked a few days ago. I think she's dying.'

Madam swore again. 'I can't have her here. You've already stirred up trouble with that white Catholic woman. If she dies here, then it will bring big trouble.'

Panic rose up in Patience's gut.

'Where can we go?'

Madam shook her head. 'I will find you a new flat. You never mention her or me, OK? Ever? If you get caught, you don't say where you stayed or who you know. Understand?'

'Yes.'

'OK. Someone will come for her this afternoon. You clean up this place after, and tomorrow I'll get you moved to the new flat. OK?'

Patience nodded.

'Do you have my money?'

Patience went to her room and found the money she had made for their debt payments. What did Madam mean that someone would come for Florence? What would they do with her and why was she separating them?

'Where will you take Florence?'

'Not your concern now. I'll sort it.'

With that Madam left, unable to stand the stench in the flat any longer.

PATIENCE STOOD in the lull of Madam's departure and stared at her friend. They would get rid of her. She was illegal, nobody would miss her. Her family at home would be told of her death. Maybe they'd get a little money and that would be it. Florence would disappear. She'd never get to paint rich ladies' fingernails.

Patience began to rock back and forth again on her heels.

She couldn't let Florence die. She was a good friend. A good person. Florence would always look after her when they worked. They were going to get a flat of their own once Madam was paid. How could she continue working without her?

She thought of Florence's little sister back home in Edo. Florence sent her postcards of London landmarks like Buckingham Palace and the Tower of London, telling her she was working in Harrods and had gone for a ride on the London Eye. She talked of the big parks, like Hyde Park and Regent's Park, and said how much they enjoyed to walk through the trees. She told her about fish and chips and American coffee shops. It had all been lies, but Florence's eyes had shone as she wrote them.

Now Florence was dying. Her eyes were fading and soon the life would leave them altogether. Patience didn't know what to do. If she sought help for her friend, it would mean they were both sent back to Nigeria, never to pay Madam back, and both would have broken their vows. If Florence died here, never leaving, then the ancestors couldn't be angry with her and she would be able to follow them into the world of spirits.

Patience sat there humming a song to her friend, wishing they had never made this journey. Never had to spend their days being used by foreign men. There was no way out. No hope of this nightmare ending. Perhaps Florence was the lucky one.

24

The minute that their briefing broke up, Harrison took the muti samples that Robert Mbeki had given him to the forensics lab for testing. The focus of the investigation might have moved away from Themba and the juju priest, but proving what Themba was doing in the UK would undoubtedly be useful in the trial.

He pushed open one of the big grey doors to the lab and immediately spotted Tanya talking to a man in a suit. There were several people there, some bent over, looking at samples of something under a microscope; others using equipment with gloves, glasses and protective clothing on. Yet his eyes had been instantly drawn to the brunette across the room, with her long hair tied up into a figure of eight at the back of her head and pinned into place by what looked like a pencil.

She looked up at him and her professional face was instantly transformed by a smile, which electrified her eyes and sent a quivering feeling into his belly. Tanya motioned to him that she'd be five minutes. He nodded and waited.

While he stood there, Harrison tried to scientifically

rationalise the feeling that he was experiencing. At its most basic animal instinct, testosterone was obviously responsible for the lust, but it was far more complicated than that. He knew that falling in love had nothing to do with his heart; it was his brain. Deep inside his temporal lobes was the limbic system, and that's where his hypothalamus sat, and where the chemicals which created the feeling he had right now were being produced. The attraction he felt towards Tanya was like a drug.

Dopamine, for sure, was one cause. That was the feel-good chemical which was released whenever he did anything that gave him pleasure. Then there was norepinephrine, which was activated in times of stress. Together, these two hormones gave him the feeling of euphoria when he saw Tanya. Too much of them and they might affect his appetite and sleep. Plus, there was the impact his attraction to her had on his serotonin, reducing its levels. Serotonin moderates his appetite and moods – which could explain why he felt a compulsion to be around her.

He watched as Tanya absentmindedly brushed a lock of hair from her face. She was concentrating on the conversation she was having, oblivious to his raging chemicals.

Harrison knew that these same chemicals also reduced his critical thinking and self-awareness. It was one reason why he'd tried to avoid relationships for so long. If he detached himself from her now, ended their affair, then he might avoid the final stage of love, which is attachment, when oxytocin and vasopressin are released. Bonding hormones that would make their relationship a long-term feeling which ran deeper and became even harder to suppress. The idea of it made him nervous, wary. Thoughts of loss loomed in his mind, but still he stayed rooted to the spot, watching the beautiful woman across the room and craving her closeness.

Tanya shook hands with the person she'd been talking to. He was a man in a suit and tie, slickly presented with body language that was all about pleasing and assisting Tanya. For a few seconds, Harrison had thought he was hitting on his girlfriend, but thankfully his rational thinking kicked back in, and he'd realised he was merely a salesman using his persuasive techniques.

They walked towards Harrison, and the man left the way he'd come in.

'Hello, stranger, lovely to see you.' Tanya smiled at him. She furtively glanced around the room at her colleagues, who were all concentrating on whatever they were doing, and then stood on her tiptoes and kissed his lips.

The kiss tingled all the way down to his toes.

'Sorry about the hold-up. He was from the forensics lab we outsource to. It's an important relationship so I needed to speak to him.'

'That's fine. I didn't have an appointment,' Harrison replied.

Tanya smiled at him.

'So what you got for me?'

'Muti, African medicines. I need to know if there are any human remains in them, or if they're all plant based.'

'OK, that shouldn't take too long for an initial analysis. Is this linked to the other bones that were brought in relating to the black magic case?'

'Yes, the divination bones. Any results yet?'

'All animals. A mixture of goat, dog, lion, and some kind of deer species.'

'Good, that's a big relief. I'm hoping we can finalise things if these are plant-based.'

'No problem, I could get these quickly processed for you in return for your company over dinner?'

'Well, that seems a small price to pay.' Harrison smiled into her eyes. They drew him down and into her personal space, where he could smell her hair and feel her warm breath on his skin. It was his turn to look around the room to ensure no eyes were watching. Then he bent and met her lips with his, savouring their touch. He wrenched himself away. 'I have to get going. I've been neglecting all my other work, trying to deal with this one case. Text me when you're thinking I might need to repay you for your services.'

His fingers trailed behind him, betraying the reluctance with which he left, and craving the touch of her hand until the last moment. Then, with one final backwards glance, he sighed and headed to the car park and his bike. There was work to be done.

It was good to get back to their office and find Ryan in residence. While working alone in peace was usually his preferred status, Harrison had grown accustomed to Ryan's presence.

'Morning, boss,' Ryan cheerfully greeted him as he pushed open the door.

'Ryan. How did the packing go?'

'Really good, actually. Quite cathartic. Chucked loads of stuff out and have a couple of bin bags full of charity shop stuff to go. They won't collect, so would you mind if we dropped them off on the way to the new place?'

'Of course, no problem.' Harrison wondered how somebody who didn't go shopping could have so much stuff to get rid of, but he guessed Ryan was a big online shopper. He used to wear the classic computer geek uniform of hoody and trainers, but lately Harrison had noticed Ryan seemed to be taking his style tips from Elon Musk. Although he wouldn't have chosen the same designer labels, the effect was still the same. His everyday attire was usually a black or white crew neck T-shirt, with classic indigo-blue straight leg jeans. Critically, Ryan had taken to wearing black leather Oxfords on his feet, and occasionally he'd even worn a white shirt. Elon's style was a cut above Ryan's original Mark Zuckerberg phase of signature grey t-shirt, trainers and jeans that the Facebook founder had worn virtually every day for the past decade.

Harrison wasn't sure what Ryan's grade rise in tech billionaire fashion was related to. He hoped it was a sign of Ryan's growing confidence and belief in his own skills. When they'd first met, the young techie certainly wouldn't have bothered about what he was wearing.

'Saw the reports about the Mannings. Both dead,' Ryan said, closely watching his boss with a look of hope on his face. He knew the whole back story.

Harrison humphed.

'So you don't believe it?' Ryan ventured.

'I believe she's dead. We knew she was dying anyway, but him? No.'

Harrison sat down on top of his desk, planting his feet on the floor and facing Ryan.

'So what's his game plan?'

'To discredit me.'

Ryan raised his eyebrows.

'They've already got Harrogate police investigating Freda's disappearance from the hospice. I was officially the last person to visit, but obviously he got in there somehow to get her out. Then, a couple of nights ago, I had my bike helmet snatched. Young guy on a stolen pizza delivery moped. I can guarantee you that my DNA is somehow going to turn up at the murder scene, at the very least. He helped Freda, gave her a huge dose of morphine to put her out of her pain. Then he probably killed someone to make it look like it had been him who died with her. All of that he's going to try to pin on me.'

'Shit,' Ryan helpfully replied.

'Mmhm. And that doesn't take into account the fact they might be also trying to link me to the murder of Annette Ward in 1993.'

'You were only like six or seven years old!'

'Yeah, I appreciate they won't bring a murder charge against me, but it could put me there. It raises questions. Throws suspicion on my character.'

'Surely whoever is SIO will try to trace Desmond and find out he's still alive?'

Harrison shook his head. 'They think his body is the pile of charcoal and ash near to Freda's. They have no reason to believe he's alive.'

'OK, then we fight back. What's the plan?'

Harrison appreciated that Ryan had used the word *we* and not just *you*.

'Thanks, Ryan. He's made a big mistake. He's shown himself. Up to now, they'd kept themselves completely in the shadows. We've never known where to look for them. But by doing all this, he's left us a trail. A trail that we can now track. If we can find out where that pizza delivery rider went, then that could lead us to Desmond.'

'I'm on it.' Ryan instantly turned his focus back to his screens, to the skills he'd mastered. 'What time did you say he snatched the helmet?'

'But we have to prioritise other cases first.' Harrison held his hand up. 'I'm concerned about the two women that Anne Francis was trying to help. Nobody is looking for them because the focus of the investigation is elsewhere now. They're victims of ritualistic crime and so they're our responsibility. Perhaps we might be able to track Anne's movements, see where she met them. Find out where they are working or live? There could be two women out there who need our help.'

Harrison had just settled down to sorting out his long list of unread emails when a text came through from Tanya.

> Good news, all plant matter. Not even any
> animal proteins.

That *was* good news, and further evidence that Themba was totally innocent. He relayed the information to Jack.
Jack immediately messaged back.

> Running out of ideas as to cause of illness.

Harrison could hear the frustration in Jack's words. There were still so many unanswered questions. He sent back:

> You called in Public Health?

> Yes, they're testing water at church.

It wasn't the water, Harrison knew that. There had to be another cause that was rooted in the church, but what? He grabbed his jacket and new helmet and headed back over to Lewisham.

25

Harrison arrived in the incident room just as Jack's mobile started to ring.

'DS Salter,' he answered.

'Cotton top. Got an update for you.' Jack looked at Harrison, who had just come to stand next to his desk and motioned that he needed five minutes to deal with the phone call. This was a conversation he didn't want to have in front of Harrison. Instead, he walked quickly to the meeting room and shut the door.

'Go for it, Gordon.'

'Right, we could be on to a suspect. We managed to trace back to where Desmond Manning was living. It was a bedsit, paid up to the end of the month. There's evidence of a struggle, some blood on the carpet in the living room. But we've found a motorcycle helmet. The perp must have forgotten it when he drove the Mannings in their car to the murder scene. Might get this wrapped up in record time if they're on the database.'

'Motorbike helmet?'

'Yup, and it's an unusual design, too. They only sell them in one or two shops in London, so we could track him that way as well. If we get a name, I'll let you know. See if it ties up to your historic inquiries.'

Jack had stopped breathing, and his heart was racing.

'Great. Thanks for letting me know. Are you any closer to confirming if the other body is Desmond's?'

'We've no reason to assume it's not. Blood at his flat and all the other evidence. We've obviously got Forensics on the case, but I'm thinking it's him and we have someone out there who wanted them both dead.'

Jack sat in the meeting room for a few moments, trying to bring his breathing and heart back under control. Harrison had lost his helmet. He had motive. He was up in Harrogate when Freda went missing. Everything pointed to him.

He stood up and looked out the meeting room window into the main office. Harrison had been netted by his groupies. Rachel, Meera, and PC Jackie Corbett were all crowded round listening to him as though it was some kind of Cbeebies' bedtime story hour.

Suddenly Jack saw red and marched over to the meeting room door, flinging it open, and heading straight for Harrison, who was giving a mini lecture on African sangomas.

'They see illness differently to us. It's not just a physical effect, but one caused by supernatural or spiritual misalignment. Treatments have been developed over centuries using natural and mystical properties. Themba was treating Robert Mbeki's arthritis with coral tree bark, and bitter aloe, or aloe vera. They're natural anti-inflammatories. Traditional healers like Themba are legally recognised and widely consulted in South Africa...'

'Dr Lane.'

Jack's voice came out hard and loud. It surprised even

himself. He could hear the controlled anger and so could Harrison, and the three female police officers who all looked up at him, shocked. Even some of the other officers around them lifted their heads from whatever they were working on to look.

'Jack!' Harrison replied a little warily. Totally confused by the sudden change in attitude of his friend.

'I need to speak to you,' Jack replied. His jaw was tense, his lips thin, and there was a slight colour in his cheeks showing the anger that was burning inside him.

'Sure,' Harrison replied calmly and walked over to the meeting room with Jack close on his heels.

Jack almost slammed the door closed.

'Why were you buying a new helmet?' The words almost growled out of him.

'Mine was stolen,' Harrison replied.

Jack detected a defensiveness in his tone.

'Stolen! Have you been playing me like a fool?' Jack walked up to Harrison, bringing his shoulders back and his chest out. The jugular vein in his neck was pulsing.

'I've no idea what you're talking about, Jack.'

'I've had the SIO on the Manning murder case on the phone, telling me they've found a motorbike helmet that sounds remarkably like it could be yours, at the home address of Desmond Manning.'

'Mine was stolen, Jack. It was snatched by a moped rider two nights ago, before the so-called murders.'

Jack glowered at him.

'I told you they were planning something. They are trying to discredit me. To ruin my reputation. Do you seriously believe that the charred remains in that fire are Desmond Manning? Don't you think it's just a little bit too convenient that the body can't be identified?'

'Not what the SIO thinks.'

'Come on, Jack. You know what's been going on.'

Neither man had realised that their voices had risen, and it hadn't gone unnoticed in the incident room. They were oblivious to the faces turned towards them, the raised eyebrows and the inquisitive expressions.

'I know what I think, Harrison. I think you wanted them dead. That you think they murdered your mother – and I accept they may well have. But what I see is an awful lot of coincidences and God help me, but if you've been lying to me...'

As he said it, Jack jabbed him aggressively in the chest.

Instantly Harrison grew several inches and his muscles tensed, ready to fight.

Jack sensed the change and the two men squared up to each other like angry stags. Harrison could have decked him with one blow – Jack was shorter and nowhere near as proficient a fighter as him, and they both knew it.

Harrison took a step back.

'I swear to you, Jack, that I did not touch either of them. I didn't take Freda. I didn't kill her, and I've never been to wherever it is that her charred remains were found. My helmet was stolen. I've reported it. End of. They are vindictive, nasty individuals and for some reason he wants to see me ruined.'

Harrison had just got his last words out when the door burst open and a furious DCI Sandra Barker walked into the room.

'What the hell is going on in here?' she hissed at them both, closing the door behind her.

Jack and Harrison were still standing squared up in front of each other. Her voice broke the tension that had seemed to hold them fixed, and as they looked up, they saw the audience outside in the incident room turn away.

'Well?' DCI Barker repeated, 'I've just had a panicked colleague come into my office thinking that you, Jack, are about to be slaughtered by the Incredible Hulk here.'

'It's all right, ma'am,' Jack said, resorting to showing that he respected her authority by not calling her Sandra. 'We were just discussing a personal matter.'

Sandra Barker looked from one man to the other. The flushed faces and tension were evident; you could almost smell the testosterone in the room.

'You discuss your personal matters in your own time, but I'm glad to hear that you're not so damned stupid that you think you'd be able to get the better of Harrison,' she said, raising an eyebrow.

Both men had backed down and threw a glance at each other.

'I've just heard that there's been another death within the St Mary's congregation: a ninety-four-year-old who presented with flu. Could be coincidence, but you two should be concentrating on this case, not banging heads in here about personal issues? I thought you'd both grown out of that ages ago.'

Jack shook himself out of the trance he'd been in.

'Sorry, boss, let me get some of the rest of the team in and we'll fill you in on where we're at.' He gave a hard stare to Harrison, who sat himself down at the table.

HARRISON COULDN'T BLAME Jack for his reaction. If he wasn't on the receiving end of the Mannings' poison, then he'd have been pretty incredulous that two people could be so evil and scheming. Yet Jack had been the one to believe in him in the first place. Had he lost that trust?

Jack opened the door to the briefing room, letting the tension flow out and the rest of the team to come in. None of them had done any work in the last fifteen minutes anyway, so they were ready and waiting. They piled in, looking from Jack to Harrison for any signs as to what the altercation had been about and who had been the victor. Neither gave anything away.

Jack took the lead with the briefing, behaving as though he was trying to redeem himself in front of Sandra. Harrison sat silently, struggling to regain his concentration. The face of Anne and the others who were ill coming up on the screen in front of them made Harrison pull himself back. He was determined he wasn't going to let the Mannings distract him. He had to give his all to this case and get justice for those who were unable to fight for it themselves.

Jack updated Sandra. 'Following the forensics analysis of the ash the juju priest blew onto Anne, we are proceeding with our assumption that her death was unrelated to his so-called curse. Whether the allegation being placed on the juju priest is a deliberate attempt to deflect blame, and possibly has a racial motive, or is an accidental coincidence, we don't yet know.

'What we are focusing on is her manner of death and the disposal of her body, particularly in connection with the potential motive of the inheritance. We're tracing all CCTV that might show us who visited Anne at her home in the days leading up to her death, plus looking through church and personal finances.'

'What about the other people falling ill? Are you saying that's just a coincidence too?' DCI Barker questioned.

'No. There's clearly something or somebody infecting the

congregation, and it's not being spread through contact with already infected individuals. We're ruling out an environmental issue. Still waiting on Public Health to see if they've found anything wrong with the water at the church, but prelims are clear.'

'So, for all intents and purposes, if you're a believer, then it seems like this voodoo curse is real. That gives somebody a racial motive, doesn't it?'

'Possibly.'

'Suspects, then?'

'John Bellamy and Stephen Chase have been in prison and yet people are still falling ill, so that could potentially put them in the clear, but we've not ruled them out.'

'They could have been working with someone else at the church. Someone who has been administering whatever it is.'

'The sacrament!' DC Oaks said. Everyone turned to look at him. 'You know, the blood of Christ and all that: the wine and bread that the priest gives out.'

'Communion,' Harrison added.

'Yeah. Everyone goes up and the priest gives them a sip of wine and some bread or a wafer or something. Maybe that's contaminated somehow, and that's how they fall sick?'

'Good shout, DC Oaks. Get them tested,' DCI Sandra Barker said to him. 'And how sure are we that Father Wilson is on the level?' she asked the room.

The team looked at each other. Jack answered for them.

'He's cooperated. But he gave the order for Anne to be cremated, which conveniently means we can't verify cause of death. The motive could be her bequest and saving the church. But why make others ill? If that was the reason, then surely things would have quietened down.'

'It comes back to the racial motive again. How to provoke community violence. Have a congregation of elderly white

Catholics falling victim to a black magic curse. It's textbook incitement with brainwashing and propaganda,' said DCI Barker. 'Let's map the relationships of those who are getting sick. Is there some common individual within the church that they all have interactions with, besides Father Wilson? And look into him again, he wouldn't be the first killer priest.'

'On it,' Jack said, the relief to be talking about the case and putting the earlier 'incident' behind him evident on his face. He threw another look at Harrison, who gave him a steady, unmoving gaze in return.

26

J ack was still talking to some of the team about what he needed them to be working on when DC David Oaks burst back into the briefing room.

'Just had Terry Dukes from Vice on, said they're about to bust the sex-trafficking ring and thought we'd like to join them seeing as we'd flushed them out.'

Jack's eyebrows shot up. 'I was wondering when that one would come home to roost. So we could finally get our two women from the church... Did he give any clues as to whether the juju priest might be among them?'

David shook his head. 'They were literally on their way to the bust and he couldn't talk for long.'

'OK. It's worth us talking to them. They spent time with Anne just before she died. Perhaps she confided in them. We'd better get going now before they ship them all out and they get dispersed around the country.'

. . .

En route, Jack was grateful that David was tactful enough not to bring up his altercation with Harrison earlier, or ask what it was about. It was still niggling him. Harrison had disappeared at the end of the briefing and so they'd not had the opportunity to finalise things. He had at least calmed down from earlier – and maybe having some space between them right now was a good thing.

Only issue was, if they found their two women and the juju priest, they might have to call on Harrison for his expertise.

Jack and David drove along, mostly in silence. Both of them were tired, and hoping that this might give them the breakthrough they needed to work out how Anne might have fallen sick.

They were making good time until they got to the Old Kent Road, where roadworks had caused a traffic jam that looked like it was going to become an epic in the annuls of commuter horror stories. Jack made the decision to put the blue lights on and swung past the jams, dodging ongoing traffic.

Driving at speed in London finally woke up his adrenaline, and it was the perfect antidote to the anger and frustration he'd been feeling over the case and the situation with Harrison. He weaved in and out of the traffic at high speed, adeptly avoiding a construction lorry and giving way to a cyclist. Even after they'd passed the Old Kent Road traffic jam, he kept the lights on. It was exhilarating being back in complete control of something, using accelerator, brake, clutch, and brain to deftly negotiate the obstacles.

It wasn't until he saw David's white-knuckled hand on the dashboard that he realised maybe he'd been overdoing it a little. He looked over at his DC sitting in the passenger seat and realised he looked a little green around the gills.

'Sorry, mate,' he said, feeling a little guilty. 'Just trying to get us there on time.'

David merely muttered some kind of confirmation back and Jack decided that was probably enough of an adrenaline rush for one day and slowed them down. He couldn't say the same for David, but Jack felt a whole lot better.

WHEN THEY REACHED THE ADDRESS, the whole area was swarming with police officers. Vice had come out in force. They never knew just what kind of resistance they were going to meet when busting people-trafficking rings like this, and so firearms officers were also on scene as a precaution. Two ambulances were in attendance and they could see one of the crews was talking to a woman who was lying on a stretcher in the back of the ambulance with a drip attached.

Jack jumped out of the car and noticed David was a little slow to follow. He saw him get out, brush down his suit and take a few deep breaths before following in Jack's wake.

First off, Jack peered into the ambulance at the woman before she was taken away. He saw a pale, skinny arm hanging down from the stretcher.

The properties that had been raided were off limits while Forensics went in, but that didn't matter. It was in a repurposed gym hall next door that Jack could see the main action was taking place. He and David showed their badges to the officer manning the door, and he alerted Terry Dukes that they'd arrived.

They weren't allowed to go inside without a chaperone, so while they waited for Terry, they stood in the doorway and surveyed the operation. It was slick and reminded Jack of the big halls that had been turned into vaccination centres during the covid crisis. Makeshift cubicles had been set up and various agencies were busy processing the women who milled around in the middle like frightened deer, clasping blankets and bottles of water.

Jack shook his head at the scene.

'Sickening, isn't it? Every one of these women was desperate and trying to improve their lot in life, and look where they ended up: in a shithole in London servicing men so that somebody else could get rich.'

David sighed next to him.

Jack realised he'd still not said a word.

'You all right, mate?'

'Yeah, yeah, fine.'

'You're getting some colour back at least.' Jack smirked.

David pulled a face back at him. 'You were lucky you didn't get my rainbow salad all over you and your car. If I'd have known you liked colour so much, maybe I wouldn't have made so much effort to hold back,' he said sarcastically.

Jack took the complaint and the sarcasm. He deserved it.

A young Asian officer walked up to the pair of them. 'You here from Lewisham?' he asked.

'Yeah,' Jack replied. The guy had the most amazing big brown eyes. He looked like he could have come off a modelling shoot or film set, not be standing in the middle of a vice bust.

'Terry's over here,' the officer continued.

David and Jack followed him, heading through the hallway to a side room where DI Terry Dukes was looking over a list on a clipboard. Terry was not a man who looked like he'd just come off a modelling shoot. He was a craggy-faced northerner who had clearly enjoyed smoking and drinking in his lifetime, and sported a scar across his chin which he told everyone had been received in the line of duty, but was in fact the result of being totally inebriated and falling flat on his face on a stone floor. Since then, he'd embraced healthy living and given up the cancer sticks, but his face was a record of his past.

David took the lead, walking forward and offering his hand.

'DC Oaks,' he said.

'Good to see you,' Dukes replied. 'I thought I should let you see if your two girls are here seeing as your Soho visit enabled us to net this lot.'

'About that,' Jack interrupted. 'Any reason why you got us to make the visit?'

'Between you and me, and no further, we believed we had an informant in our team. Someone who was letting Layla know what our intel was. I needed an outside investigation, so that she was sufficiently worried to warn her girlfriend in there that there might be a whole load of coppers sniffing around. You conveniently came along and helped me out. Scratched both our backs as we knew there was a big sex-trafficking ring working around this area, and you were looking for one.'

'Did you get your mole?' Jack asked.

'I'm afraid I did.' Dukes said regretfully. 'Now, I can't spare you much time. These women need medical attention. Many of them are addicts, as you'll appreciate that's how scum like her control them.'

He nodded again at the woman in the other room. 'She'd had them locked up across the road there for months. We're assessing them and then they'll be sent to various locations depending on needs.' He consulted his clipboard. 'Looks like we've got seven Nigerian women, although one is being attended to by the ambulance crew. I'll take you through.'

Jack and David followed his lead.

Most of the women were now sitting in groups around the hall. They'd had coloured bands put around their wrists, depending on where the assessing medics and social workers had thought they'd be best looked after.

'These women are victims. We're doing our best to give them back some dignity,' Terry said as they walked. 'They've endured a lot and are still very frightened and don't trust us yet, so we need to go easy on them.'

'Where are they mostly from?' David asked now.

'All over, Romania, Asia, and Africa. They'd have made the journey to Europe and then been chosen and shipped over here from there.'

'Some of them look so young.'

'Yup. We get a fair amount of minors, but most of them are young women. Younger than you. The traffickers know what their punters like.'

They'd reached a group of five African women, and Terry stopped a few feet away.

Jack and David studied the faces that returned their gaze, trying to smile reassuringly at them. They were frightened faces that had lost all hope of being rescued. Jack took his phone out and brought up the grainy image from outside the church, then flicked through to another CCTV shot of Anne and the two women walking on their way to the church. None of the women in front of them looked like their pair. Jack shook his head.

Terry peered over their shoulders.

'No. OK, we've got two more. One's over here, but to be honest, I don't think she's one of yours either, looking at that photo.'

They walked to the other side of the hall, where a long-limbed African woman had curled herself up into a corner on a bench. One of the team was talking to her, and she was crying. Jack could see instantly she wasn't one of the women they were looking for and he didn't want them distressing her further. He felt like a dirty voyeur here, witnessing the misery and hopelessness of these women.

'It's not her,' he said simply.

Terry nodded. 'OK, last one should be with an ambulance crew.'

The pair of them followed him out of the hall and back into the night.

'Did you pick up any men?' Jack asked.

'Yup, six, but they're all Caucasian, Romanian, or British. No African men.'

Disappointment had started to sink in already. The last woman was their final hope of tracking down the trio outside of the church with Anne.

They walked towards the bright lights of the second ambulance where the crew were loading a woman in a wheelchair into the van. She had a blanket wrapped around her and her head hung down.

As they got closer, they could see that she'd been treated for a cut to her leg, and that she was younger than their church pair. Probably no more than sixteen or seventeen years old. Jack's heart went out to her. She looked like the daughter of one of their neighbours, but the needle marks on her thin arm and the look in her eyes put her a million miles away from her safe, comfortable life.

'It's not her,' he said to Terry.

'What will happen to them all?' David asked.

'First off, they'll all get medical help. Then we'll hand them over to Immigration, who'll process them all as asylum seekers. Some will get to stay, some will go back, but at least they're free now. I've got a nineteen-year-old daughter. Every time I look into each of these women's faces, I see hers. So I'm sorry you didn't find your two, but real glad you were able to help us put an end to the living hell for all of these girls.'

27

John Bellamy was very careful that he wasn't being followed. He left his house and walked along the road before turning up a small lane in between a row of properties. An ambulance had taken Margaret to hospital just half an hour ago. He'd had to make one phone call and things were already rolling. He was so angry right now that he could almost feel his blood boiling. Like a pressure cooker, he needed to vent.

He walked to the end of the lane and then stood to one side behind a fence for a few minutes, waiting to see if anyone was tracing his footsteps. He could hear a couple of dogs barking playfully up ahead on the common, and in the house behind him, a television was blaring out some afternoon quiz show he didn't recognise.

When nobody appeared around the lane's fence, he moved from his position and peered along it. Nothing. John continued with his route, walking across the common and towards the old bandstand on the far side.

As he neared, he could already see several shadowy

figures floating around its edges. His stomach tumbled and twisted with excitement. This was real. This was happening. They were going into battle and first up was the man who had caused all the misery, the crazy witch doctor who was currently languishing in the same hospital as his poor wife. How could anybody justify that? The cause of his wife's suffering, Anne's killer – not to mention the others at the church – being treated in luxury on taxpayer's money. That man was going to pay for what he'd done. Today was his reckoning.

28

The altercation with Jack had disturbed Harrison. He could understand how it looked: exactly as the Mannings had wanted it to, with him right smack bang in the middle of it all. Yet he hoped Jack had believed him.

Harrison had just left the incident room, deciding that it would be best for the inquiry if he wasn't on Jack's mind by being under his nose, when his mobile rang. It was Ryan.

'Alright, boss? I think I've found the two women who Anne was trying to help.'

'Really? Brilliant work, how and where?'

'So I tracked Anne's movements for the two months before she died. CCTV was a bit patchy in some places as it gets deleted, but I found enough. She kept going to the same area, and it's a known red-light district. Then I started to see her with the same woman, sometimes two women. It was just a case of tracking them down then. No signs of your juju guy, but I'll WhatsApp you over a photograph of them. Bit grainy, but it will help. I don't have a number for where they're living, but I do have a road; you'll find them.'

'Ryan, you get better with every day. Thank you,' Harrison said, and he meant it.

HARRISON DROVE around the red-light district first, checking to see if the women were working. He couldn't see them. Of course, they could have a client, but, either way, they weren't available for a chat.

He rode on to the address where Ryan believed they lived. It was a rundown area, built in the 1960s and definitely past its best. There was a mix of residential houses, two-up two-downs, and a small row of dingy shops – a small independent supermarket with its windows protected by thick wire mesh, a bookmaker, and a fish and chip shop – with flats above them. The buildings had some kind of pebbledash coating on them, which he could only describe as a shitty shade of brown. It summed up the street nicely.

Harrison parked his bike in the most public place he could find and stood looking around him. He perhaps should have called this in to the incident room and had Jack or David with him, but in reality he knew they'd stick out as police like sore thumbs, and he'd get nowhere with getting information from people.

He could approach this in several ways. He could just loiter and hope to see one of the women heading off for their shift or heading home. He could start systematically knocking on doors. Or he could ask around and see if anyone knew them. In the end, Harrison decided he needed some kind of prop to help break the ice and so he headed into the supermarket to buy a packet of cigarettes.

The little shop was stacked to the ceiling with various

household necessities, all at rock-bottom prices it appeared. Harrison went straight to the counter where a young woman was standing looking bored out of her mind.

'Twenty Marlboro Lights please,' Harrison said, and then nearly choked when she told him the price. He swiped his card and bought them.

'I'm looking for a couple of friends of mine, don't suppose you know where they live, do you? They told me the road but I've totally forgotten the number. Both Nigerian women, one of them has braided hair, the other's is cut short.'

The young woman's eyes narrowed, and she looked Harrison up and down. She clearly didn't like what she saw because she shook her head.

He left the shop. It was going to be tough persuading people to tell him anything. He needed to get smarter.

Harrison returned to his bike and half sat, half stood leaning on the seat, pretending to look at his mobile phone. In reality, he was scanning each person that walked past. A thin woman pushing a double buggy appeared from round the corner, and Harrison decided she had the face of a smoker. As she came alongside him, he asked for a light.

She stared right at him and carried on walking. Harrison wasn't sure if she'd heard.

'Don't suppose you've got a light, have you?' he tried again.

She turned away from him and walked faster up the road.

Harrison sighed.

'You after a light, bro?' It was a young guy in a baseball cap, hoody, and jogging pants.

'Yeah. You got one?'

The young guy reached into his pocket and pulled out a tatty plastic lighter. He chucked it to Harrison. Unfortunately, it now meant that Harrison had to light his cigarette, even though he didn't smoke. He managed to do so without taking too much smoke down and coughing, and chucked the lighter back to the young guy who was standing there eyeing him curiously.

'Want a smoke?' Harrison asked him, offering the opened packet.

'Yeah, cheers,' the guy said and reached over to take one.

'You live round here?' Harrison asked him as he lit up.

'Yeah, just down the road.'

'You might know my mates then. Two Nigerian women, one's got hair in braids, the other has her hair short.'

'Oh yeah, yeah, seen them. You's not their…'

Harrison shook his head quickly to head off the question.

'Just mates. They're supposed to be meeting me here about ten minutes ago. Not like them to be late – but you know women.'

'Yeah, yeah. They shouldn't be long seein' as they only live up there.' The guy nodded to the window above the fish and chip shop at the end of the little row of shops.

'Bet they're trying to decide what to wear,' Harrison quipped. He left it a good few moments, watching the guy take a drag from his cigarette.

'You know what, I think I might go chase them up. We've got a movie to catch.' He dropped his cigarette on the floor and ground it out.

'Good idea, bro,' the guy replied, starting to move off.

'Hey, why don't you take the rest of these?' Harrison said, throwing him the pack of cigarettes. 'I'm supposed to be giving up.'

'Sick, bro,' the guy said with a big grin on his face.

. . .

THE KNOCK on the door brought Patience out of her trance. She was tired, really tired, but she hadn't left Florence's side. She'd been falling asleep, waking herself up, swaying as she nearly fell from her kneeling position. In front of her, Florence was unchanged. The sweat glistening in the light from the hallway.

Whoever was at the door knocked again. Patience knew the Madam's men had come for her friend. For a few moments she contemplated not opening the door, but she'd seen what those men did to women like her who disobeyed them. It would take them seconds to get the front door down, and then they would deal with her just like any other obstruction. Patience let go of Florence's limp hand and went to open the door.

As she opened it, she saw a big, tall, muscular man in black leather. He didn't look like one of Madam's men, but he didn't look like police. She hesitated.

'Hi,' he said to her, 'My name is Dr Harrison Lane. I'm with the Metropolitan police.'

Patience tried to slam the door quickly, but he'd already expected her reaction and had his foot, then shoulder, pushing back against her. She panicked, running back down the hallway, although to where she didn't know. It was a dead end.

'Please don't be scared,' Harrison said, entering the flat and closing the door behind him. 'I'm here because I know Anne Francis was trying to get you some help. I don't want to hurt you, I want to help you.'

Patience thought her heart was going to burst right out of her chest.

'Anne is alive?' she asked him.

He shook his head.

'No, I'm afraid she died. Are you alone here?'

The stench of impending death filled the flat and it was obviously not coming from Patience.

'Florence.' Patience nodded to the room behind him.

Harrison peered into the room, having to wait a few seconds before his eyes could adjust to the darkness. He couldn't see clearly, but what he saw was enough. He dialled 999 immediately and asked for the ambulance service.

BY THE TIME Madam's men came to collect poor Florence, the street was filled with flashing blue lights. An ambulance and two police cars were parked by the little row of shops. The men drove straight past and dialled Madam to give her the bad news.

HARRISON CALLED Jack the moment he was able to, which was when backup had arrived and he'd been able to calm an extremely agitated Patience. He'd had to stand in the hallway blocking her exit, not daring to go into the bedroom and check on the other woman because it would give her an escape route. Her friend was obviously very ill, and Harrison hoped the ambulance wouldn't take long.

By the time Jack was on scene, Harrison was sitting with Patience in a police car. The ambulance had taken Florence away, but there was no sitting room area in their flat, and besides, the smell in there was choking and he knew Forensics would need to go in.

Harrison got out of the car and went to talk to Jack as he saw him pull up.

'Why didn't you tell us you were going in here?' Jack said to him.

Harrison heard the accusation in Jack's voice, the fear that his trust was misplaced and Harrison was a loose cannon.

'I wouldn't have been able to find them if I had. Nobody round here would have talked to a police officer, and you know as well as I do they can spot one a mile off.'

Harrison was still in his bike leathers, but the jacket was undone. He definitely didn't look like a police officer. He looked more like a bodyguard or bouncer, or somebody who worked for the wrong side of the tracks.

'So what did you find?' Jack asked, softening his tone.

'Our two women from outside the church. Patience, still not got her surname from her, is in the car. She's terrified of reprisals from the woman she calls Madam. She sponsored Patience's trafficking and Patience owes her £50k.'

'Fifty thousand? She's going to have to do a lot of turns to pay that back.'

'Yup, exactly. It will take her years. Some of what should be the best years of her life. By the time she's done, she'll still be an illegal immigrant and unable to fully integrate into society. Or she'll be dead.

'Florence is her friend. She's now in ICU at Guy's fighting for her life. Paramedics say it's advanced sepsis. I may have been too late. She could be in vital organ shutdown, but they're doing their best for her. She's got age on her side.'

'You think her illness is related to Anne's death?'

Harrison shook his head. 'No. She'd been beaten up, and Patience told me it had been a violent punter. I believe her. Anyway, it's totally different symptoms. Medics suspect broken ribs may have punctured something, or there's some other kind of internal injury from the beating.'

'What about our juju priest?'

'Not got anything about him yet. She's exhausted and very frightened.'

'OK, well maybe Vice will help us find this madam. I'll bet she's got other girls stashed in shitholes around London, funding her lifestyle. If we find her, then we can also find our witch doctor.'

'And hopefully free more victims,' Harrison added.

'I'm just off to see Pauline Jones. She's one of Anne's needlepoint group, but doesn't appear to have been ill. We're interviewing as many of the churchgoers as we can ahead of tonight to try to find a common thread between them for why they're ill. Want to tag along?' Jack was holding out the olive branch to Harrison.

'Sure. Give me the address and I'll meet you there. I'm on my bike.'

Before he left, Harrison went into the supermarket once more and bought a bottle of water and a sandwich. The girl he'd seen earlier was still on and this time she gave him a look as if she'd trodden in dirt.

'You're lucky,' he said to her. 'Those women were being forced to sell themselves to make somebody else rich. All you have to do is take people's money and fill some shelves, but I bet you never offered to help them.'

He turned his back on her open-mouthed stare and headed back to the police car, where the frightened Patience was waiting for a caseworker to arrive and take her to a safe place to be assessed. As Harrison slipped into the back seat beside her, she shrank away from him. He put the water and sandwich on the seat between them.

'Those are for you. I know you're scared,' Harrison said to her gently, 'but you are surrounded by people who are going to help you. Madam is not a good person. She may have paid for you to come over, but she was only doing it to make money while you went out and sold yourself.'

Harrison watched a single tear escape Patience's left eye and roll down her cheek.

'I know you have made a vow to a priest back home, and that involves paying Madam back. I am going to make sure someone helps you to talk to your priest, and you are freed from that vow. You've paid more than your dues.

'Anne wanted to help you. She understood the strength of your beliefs, but she also saw that these were being used to harm you. There are organisations who will support you here and back home. I know you have no reason to trust me, you don't know me, but you did trust Anne and I will ensure that what she started is finished.'

Harrison went to leave the car, but Patience shot out a hand and touched his arm.

'Thank you,' she said.

He nodded and was gone.

29

Despite his delay leaving, Harrison still managed to arrive outside Pauline Jones's house at almost the same time as Jack. The weary-looking DS Salter was just clambering out of his car as he pulled up. It gave Harrison a pang of guilt. Was Jack's exhaustion a result just of this case, or was it the worry Harrison was causing him with the Mannings?

He'd never intended for Jack to get so involved, but now he was – and the Mannings had a habit of ensuring they got their claws into everyone they came into contact with.

Jack carried on, business as normal, as though they'd not had the altercation earlier.

'So, as I said, I'm particularly interested in Pauline because she's part of Anne's inner circle, but is the only one who hasn't been ill. What had she done differently that stopped her from getting this mystery disease, or was it just a fluke?'

Jack led the way up a pretty suburban London path to a door that had climbing roses trained around it. He knocked.

From somewhere inside, a small dog yapped and they could hear the tippety-tappety sound of its clawed feet running to the front door, shouting out its intruder alert.

There was a muffled woman's voice, and then the door was opened by a tall, grey-haired woman holding a very lively Shih Tzu.

'Mrs Jones? DS Jack Salter and this is Dr Harrison Lane. I spoke to you earlier.'

'Yes, of course, come in,' Pauline said, holding on to the wriggling dog. 'I hope you're both OK with dogs? Baxter likes to check out everyone who comes into his house. He's very friendly. Would lick you to death before he'd bite you if you were a burglar, but he's a good alarm system.'

Both men smiled at the dog.

'Absolutely fine,' Jack replied.

'Would you like a cup of tea or coffee?' Pauline asked them both as she led them into a large sitting room with a floral sofa and armchairs, apart from one large wingback which sported a plain blue upholstery.

'No, we're fine, thank you,' said Jack. He was keen to crack on.

Harrison scanned the room. It was a typical middle-class family home, with evidence of Pauline's devotion to her faith on show. There were photographs of three different children dotted around the room at various stages of growth, including wedding pictures as adults. A fortieth wedding anniversary photo frame held an image of Pauline and a large jowly man, who Harrison presumed must be her husband. There was a crucifix on the wall, and copies of the bible on display.

As the two men took seats, Pauline put Baxter down on the floor. Like a magnet, he shot over to Jack and Harrison, sniffing them.

'Please do let me know if he becomes a nuisance.' She smiled at them both. 'I'm afraid we do rather indulge him. Child surrogate since we became empty-nesters.'

'It's fine.' Jack smiled reassuringly, while tickling Baxter behind his ear. 'How long had you known Anne for?' He sat back on the sofa and pulled out a notebook, leaving Harrison to entertain Baxter.

'Gosh, must be a good fifteen years or so. It was heart-breaking when we lost her. She did so much good in our community.'

'Now, as I'm sure you're aware, there are several others from the church and your needlepoint group who have also become ill. We got involved because of the assault on a South African man, who was wrongly identified as being the juju priest who had threatened Anne after she'd tried to help two Nigerian women.'

'Yes, some people think he put a curse on our church and that's why so many are falling ill.'

'What do you believe, Mrs Jones? You knew Anne well.'

Pauline thought for a few moments. Baxter, tired of having to nag Harrison to bend down and rub his tummy, resorted to jumping up on the sofa and climbing onto his lap. All three watched as he settled onto Harrison, a small ball of cream and brown fluff on Harrison's big black, leather-clad legs. He didn't mind a bit, smiled and carried on stroking the dog.

'I don't think it's a curse, DS Salter, but I don't know what it is. I can't explain it, so I can understand why some people are calling it black magic.'

'And you had no symptoms at all like the others?'

She shook her head.

'Did the others meet up at all without you, that you're aware of? Did you miss a meeting?'

'No, and to be honest, we only all met up the once before Anne fell ill. She wanted us to make a big push to get the kneeling cushions made before Christmas and so we met at her house for coffee, and collected our wools and canvases. After that she was feeling under the weather and so the only time I saw her was when I popped in to check she was OK. We set up a rota, so that someone went in at least once every day to check she was all right and didn't need anything.'

'So you visited her when she was ill in bed?'

'Yes. Twice.'

Jack sighed.

'What about at the church? Do any of the others who you know to be ill do anything different to you?'

'There's no consistent thing between them, I'm afraid. It's not just those of us in the needlepoint group. I wish I could help, but I know of six people who are definitely ill and I couldn't say what linked them other than that they visit the church regularly. Do you think it's contagious?'

'Well, it doesn't appear to be, in that people who have come into contact with sick members of the congregation haven't then fallen ill. At the moment, all we can assume is that the source of the illness is the church. Public Health is investigating.'

It was Pauline's turn to sigh.

'I must get back to my needlepoint. I had to stop awhile because I was overdoing it and developed some blisters on my fingers which made it quite painful.' Pauline showed them her hands, which did indeed look sore. There were dried red blisters with black centres dotted around her fingers, palm side. 'I've been scratching them so I think I've made them worse,' she added.

Pauline absentmindedly picked up a basket by the side of

her chair which contained a plastic pot, a plastic bag of wool, and an unfinished canvas.

'Baxter did his best to stop me from my needlework, too. He's worse than a cat. Has the wool out all over the place. It's only since I found this old plastic pot that I've managed to stop him.' Pauline pulled out a mottled brown pot with wool poking out of a hole in the top. 'Looks a bit old-fashioned, I know, but it does the job. He gets most frustrated that he can't reach it.' She smiled at her dog, who was still sitting, looking more than comfortable, on Harrison's lap.

'If you think of anything else that might help us identify the cause of this illness, please do get in touch, won't you?' Jack said to her, rising from the sofa.

Harrison lifted a disappointed Baxter off his legs and followed Jack.

ONCE OUTSIDE, they had a quick debrief.

'I take it from the fact you didn't ask any questions, you didn't spot any connections?'

Harrison shook his head. 'No. If it was just the needle-point group, then you'd have an easier job of it, but it's not and the church is a big space. Those who fall ill seem to come from a variety of backgrounds.'

'There's no pattern,' said Jack.

'And yet there must be,' Harrison replied. 'There must be a pattern that we're just not seeing yet. One person who has contact with all the ill individuals, or something which they are all doing.'

'Well, come along to this cleansing service tonight and see if you can identify it, because I sure as hell can't right now.' Jack rubbed his hands through his hair and sighed for the fiftieth time that day.

30

The meeting room stank of pizza. A stack of empty boxes were already piled on the floor, and only a couple remained on the table with the remnants of what had once been a pizza feast courtesy of DCI Barker.

The team was poring over a diagram of the church and the victim statements they'd gathered that afternoon from those who had fallen ill.

'This is doing my bloody head in,' Geoff said.

'It's got to be here somewhere. There has to be a common denominator between all these victims, besides the church.' Jack said to him.

'Apart from Father Wilson, there's not. Some of them are in the needlepoint group, some of them aren't, and not all the people in that group are ill, anyway. The only common denominator among the non-needlepointers seems to be that they're all elderly. Could someone be practising a bit of euthanasia on the old? Have we got a religious Harold Shipman in the congregation?' Geoff replied.

'Father Wilson and some of the other church officials

administer the Communion. Perhaps there are certain wafers for the chosen ones,' DC David Oaks volunteered.

'But it's not poisoning. These people have flu symptoms.'

'Ricin apparently can give flu-like symptoms,' Geoff offered.

'So we've gone from Harold Shipman to some bloody terrorist plot with Ricin now?'

'Wouldn't be unheard of. There was that plot to hit the London Underground with Ricin back in 2003, remember?'

'OK, you're right in that we can't rule anything out, but none of it is making any bloody sense,' Jack replied.

They all fell silent and stared vacantly at the paperwork on the table.

'I don't see Margaret Bellamy's statement here,' Harrison said to the room.

'No. We're not exactly popular in that household and by the time we decided to speak to all the people who had become ill, John was out of prison. He wouldn't let us speak to her,' Jack said to him.

The door opened and DCI Barker walked in.

'Good news, everyone. They've picked up the madam running the Nigerian sex workers, and also a man called Osezua Idahosa, who happens to have dreadlocks and claims to be a juju priest. They're currently in with the vice squad team who think there's probably another half dozen victims around the capital. Once they've secured their safety, then we can get in to speak to them.'

'That is good news,' Jack replied.

'Well, I take it from the underwhelming response from the rest of you that you're still no further forward on finding out who or what is killing the St Mary's parishioners?' DCI Sandra Barker scanned the faces around the table.

'No, Ma'am,' came the muted reply.

'Is it some kind of pathogen? Do we have a more subtle form of the Salisbury Novichok incident going on?'

'Bloody hell,' muttered Jack. 'Any other conspiracy theories that people want to suggest? We haven't thought about radiation poisoning yet? Could be a Russian plot?'

DCI Barker looked at Jack with her eyebrows raised. 'Not some Coronavirus mutation, I hope?' she proffered instead.

Jack gave another one of his big sighs. 'It doesn't appear to be contagious.'

'Well, thank God for small mercies,' she replied. 'I'll leave you to it.' She glanced over at Harrison as she left, giving him a knowing smile.

HARRISON WAS SMILING INSIDE. Capturing the Madam and Osezua was a win. He wanted them punished for what they did to all the young women who were forced into sex work. What they took from the women was far more than just money. The only downside was that he knew they were just the tip of the iceberg.

'We will still need to interview the juju priest,' Jack said. 'Harrison, you're going to have to sit in on that. I doubt it's going to help us now, but we need to cross the Ts and dot the Is.'

Harrison nodded. 'Talking of which, Ryan has confirmed there's CCTV footage of Themba, which backs up his alibi. He's definitely in the clear.' Harrison told him.

The entire team had been intensely watching the interactions between Harrison and Jack throughout the afternoon. The gossip grapevine had been in full flow following their altercation, but nobody knew why. David had been quizzed nonstop, but he didn't have any more of a clue than the others. It appeared that whatever it was had been put behind them because both men seemed to be behaving as normal.

'So, the priority has to be this service tonight...'

Jack was interrupted by his mobile ringing.

'DS Salter. Yep. Mhhmm. Mmmh. OK. Thank you.'

Jack pocketed his mobile and took out his car keys.

'Margaret Bellamy has just been admitted to hospital, she hasn't been assessed yet. She's in A & E and quite poorly. She's at the epicentre of what's been going on, so I'd really like to have a word with her while she's away from the control of John. Harrison, can you come with me?

'The rest of you, I want you getting ready for tonight's service. I might be a bit late. I want someone watching every single one of those people handing out Communion. If someone there is slipping something into the wine, or anyone acts in the slightest bit suspicious, I want you on it. David, you're to track Father Wilson's every move. He's the one man who has access to everybody and everything.

'Also, we might get trouble outside, so be on your guard. If the far right start stirring up social media again, then we need to be ready. TSG is on standby and will be parked up just a few streets away in case of any issues. Good luck for tonight, all. Watch everyone closely, see who interacts with whom. There has to be the answer somewhere, staring us right in the face.'

31

Harrison tailgated Jack all the way to the hospital, and the pair of them headed straight into Accident and Emergency to find Margaret.

The hospital was the same as every other one like it up and down the country, busting at the seams with patients and filled with nurses, doctors and other support staff, all doing their absolute best to keep the ship on course. Jack hated to add to their workload, but they needed to speak to Margaret. Find out if she had any idea where she'd contracted the illness from, or who might be responsible. If there was somebody else at the church with an agenda, and perhaps with links to John, then she might be persuaded to tell them.

He managed to grab one of the A & E nurses and asked her where they could find Margaret. She pointed to a bed at the far end of the room.

'She's still waiting to see the doctor, so you'll have to leave if they arrive.'

'No problem,' Jack confirmed.

The curtain was open around Margaret's bed, and Jack

and Harrison found her lying on her back with an oxygen mask assisting her breathing. She was wired up to heart and oxygen monitors. She certainly didn't look well. Her chest heaved up and down to grasp at the air she needed to breathe.

'She looks worse than I thought,' Jack whispered to Harrison. 'This might have been a waste of time. I was hoping you could use some of your persuasive psychology techniques to get her to tell us what's going on.'

They walked up to her bed, but she still didn't open her eyes.

'Mrs Bellamy? Mrs Bellamy, we're from the police,' Jack spoke to her gently. 'We're hoping to talk to you in order to find out why you and your fellow worshippers are falling ill.'

Margaret's eyelids flickered, and then slowly opened. The whites were red, and she struggled to keep her eyes open; it was as though they were on failing hydraulics, which kept lifting and then slipping back down again.

'Mrs Bellamy, I'm sorry to have to ask you questions when you're not feeling well, but we're concerned about the cause of your illness and that of many others in your congregation.'

Margaret grasped at her oxygen mask and beckoned Jack to lean in closer.

'He's gone. He's looking for him,' she whispered.

'Whose gone?'

'John.'

'I'm sure he'll be back soon.'

'No,' she rasped. 'Stop them.'

Jack looked at Harrison to see if he had any idea what Margaret was talking about.

'Mrs Bellamy, are you saying that John has gone looking for someone?' Harrison asked.

She turned to look at him and lowered her eye lids to signal yes.

'The man who he attacked before? Themba Sisulu?'

'Yes,' she replied. 'There are others. You must stop them. He's already in trouble.' Margaret reached out with the last of her strength and pulled at Jack's sleeve.

Harrison was already halfway down the ward and heading for the stairs.

THEMBA'S ROOM was on the second floor of the hospital. Harrison didn't wait for the lift. He took the stairs, bounding up them two steps at a time. Once on the second floor, it took him just a moment to reassess his surroundings and remember where he'd visited Themba a few days earlier. He ran down the corridor, nearly colliding with the same Irish nurse who had helped them get Themba comfortable.

She shouted after him, but he didn't hear her. He was focused on one thing, and one thing only.

When he reached Themba's room, he burst straight in through the door, not worrying to think that the room might have been reassigned.

It was empty.

Harrison walked in and checked the name on the bed. It still said Themba Sisulu. There was no sign of a scuffle, and Themba's stick was gone. He checked in the bathroom to ensure John Bellamy wasn't hiding in there. Neither man was in sight. So where were they?

'What are you doing?' The Irish nurse had caught up with him by now. 'We've just been told by security that someone could be trying to harm Themba.'

'Yes. Have you seen anyone? Have you seen Themba?' Harrison asked her.

'No. He was here about half an hour ago.' She looked around the room, confused, as though expecting him to be hiding somewhere.

Harrison couldn't waste anymore time. He ran out and back down the corridor to the nurse's desk.

'Have you seen Themba?' he barked at them.

'Not recently,' one of the nurses replied, and the rest of them shook their heads. 'He wanders off sometimes.'

'Where to? Where does he go?'

'Don't know. He just comes back and won't say,' one of the nurses replied.

Harrison texted Jack: *Not in room nor ward. Keep eye on all exits, they may be taking him outside.*

Where would Themba wander off to in the hospital? Harrison racked his brains, thinking about the kind of space where a man not used to busy medical buildings would find solace.

Then Harrison remembered something that Sisulu had said to him the last time he was there: *In London there are no mountains to lift me closer to speak to my spirits.* He headed back to the stairwell and the roof.

Harrison was glad he was fit. There were more floors in the hospital than he'd bargained for, and five flights later, he eventually arrived at the final door which said: *No Entry for Unauthorised personnel.* It was clear that he wasn't the only one who ignored the sign: the door wasn't firmly closed, as though somebody else had been through it recently.

Harrison walked out onto a large space that covered the entire footprint of the main hospital building. Themba could be anywhere up here, and visibility was hampered by the numerous vents, lift shaft-winding machinery, air conditioning, and other plant machinery dotted around the roof. Harrison thought quickly, using his knowledge of

Themba's beliefs. He would face east, but which way was east?

Harrison looked at the stars. It had been a while since he'd used them to determine direction, but it was a constant that never changed. He worked out which way he was facing and turned to the right.

Harrison had covered around half of the roof space when he became aware that he wasn't alone in his search. Across the other side, he could hear the sounds of several people running, and they were heading in the same direction as Harrison. He ran faster, until he could see the edge of the eastern wall of the building, and, rising above the wall, the silhouetted top half of a man, arms raised, stick in hand. Themba was speaking to his spirits.

Harrison reached Themba just as he saw the shadows of three men come running around the side of a lift shaft. He grabbed his mobile from his pocket and dialled the last number. Harrison didn't take his eyes off the men, but as soon as he heard Jack's voice come through the earpiece, distant and tiny, he shouted to him that he was on the roof, east side, and he wasn't alone. Then he pocketed the phone and got ready.

'Stay still,' he said to Themba, who was looking confused and frightened by the sudden appearance of Harrison and the three other men heading straight for them. 'I'll protect you.' Harrison turned, planted his feet firmly, and faced the men.

John Bellamy ran into the light first.

'Dr Lane!' He stopped dead, around twenty yards from Harrison.

'Turn around, John, and walk away,' Harrison said to him calmly and with authority.

He saw John's face flicker with uncertainty, then harden.

'I won't. That witch doctor has put my wife into A & E and put a curse on my church. He has to pay for what he's done.'

'John, this isn't the man who you saw with Anne. This man's name is Themba Sisulu. He is a South African healer. He was in Anne's road, helping someone from his home village. The man you saw was a Nigerian juju priest called Osezua Idahosa. We have just arrested him. You are trying to seek vengeance against the wrong man.'

'You're lying.'

'I'm not, I promise you. And the powder the priest blew onto Anne was just ash. We've had it tested, but even if it had made Anne ill, it couldn't have hurt Margaret or any of the others. Please step away now and go back down to your wife. If you come any closer to us, then you'll be risking further imprisonment for no reason, and she needs you now.'

John hesitated and, sensing his weakening resolve, the two men behind him stepped forward into the light. They wore all black, including black face masks and beanie hats. In their gloved hands Harrison saw the silver flash of blades. Both men were fairly well built, and neither were short.

'We don't give a shit what his name is. He's in our country spreading un-Christian black magic. He needs to be taught a lesson,' the younger of the two spoke now. There was venom in his voice.

'John. You can stop this now before it goes any further. Turn around, go back to Margaret and that will be the end of this.' Harrison tried to appeal to John's better side. He could see there were doubts on his face.

While John thought about it, Harrison weighed up his chances against all three of them. John would be easy. The other two were armed and clearly not desk-bound accountants.

'There are police and security staff on their way up here now.' Harrison pushed at John's doubt.

'Then we'd better get this done quick,' the younger of the other two replied.

Harrison hadn't expected them to strike so fast, but he was ready. He was always ready.

As the two men rushed towards him, he stepped back and pinned Themba against the wall, shielding him, while at the same time reaching behind with his arms and placing his palms, backwards on the wall.

The younger man was the fastest, a few seconds ahead of the other.

Harrison stood firm until the man was just a few feet away, and then, using his arms and the wall, he levered himself up and into a double kick, planting his feet right into the centre of the man's chest, and clipping his chin as well. A grunt of shock was propelled out of the man as he flew backwards and towards his oncoming companion.

The second man only just managed to dodge being knocked over and let out a roar of rage as he headed straight for Harrison. Harrison, not moving a muscle, let him run full pelt at them.

He could see the whites of the man's eyes, the beads of sweat forming under his beanie hat.

Just two feet away from the point of the knife reaching them, Harrison turned, grabbing Themba and flinging him to one side as he, too, moved. Then, swiftly, he kicked out with his right foot.

The man, unable to stop the momentum that he'd created, headed straight for the wall, and fixated by his impending crash into it, failed to see Harrison's foot kick out and trip him so that he fell headfirst into the bricks with a sickening thud.

Harrison was satisfied his threat was neutralised, and turned, ready for the next attack from the younger man, who was already back on his feet and heading towards Harrison, shouting a string of expletives.

Behind him, Harrison heard John shouting for the man to stop and leave now, but his words had no effect.

The man approached more cautiously this time, swiping his blade in front of him, ready to cut Harrison should he dare to extend a leg or arm. Harrison pushed Themba towards the corner, where he had two walls to defend him and only one approach. Then Harrison placed himself right in the centre of that approach.

'You're going to have to get through me to get to him. Why don't you quit while you can,' Harrison said. His voice still sounded calm and authoritative, in stark contrast to the rampant, enraged screams of his two assailants.

He could see the man weighing up his chances. Harrison was in a good position to try the same manoeuvre as he'd done the first time. He could almost see the realisation dawning on the man.

'I'd call this checkmate, but I think that I'm in possession of the king, so it looks like you've lost,' he said to their attacker.

From across the roof, he could hear the sound of several pairs of feet running in their direction.

'And here's the cavalry.'

The man panicked, making a feeble attempt to throw the knife at Harrison before he spun around and ran. He didn't get far.

'Not so fast, mate,' Harrison heard, followed by a scuffle.

Jack's puffed red face came into view, flanked by a security guard and two uniformed police officers, and Harrison allowed himself to relax.

Jack beamed a huge smile when he saw Harrison and Themba standing unharmed, the slumped figure of one of the attackers on the floor beside them.

'Don't tell me they thought that two of them could take you out.' Jack laughed. 'Obviously don't know you.'

'John Bellamy was here too, but he left when the action started.'

'Don't worry about Mr Bellamy, we caught his sorry arse on the way down the stairway.'

Harrison went over to the unconscious man on the floor and felt for a pulse, finding one.

'We'll need some medical attention for this guy. He accidentally ran into the wall.'

The hospital security guard got onto his radio straight away and while the police officers bagged the two knives, Harrison helped move the man into the recovery position.

'Mr Sisulu, I'm sorry for the terrible trauma that you've had to deal with,' Jack was saying to Themba. 'This should not have happened.'

'I am a lucky man. I had my guardian to keep me safe.' Themba smiled at Harrison.

'Yes. You always want Dr Lane on your side,' Jack added, but then thought about the Mannings, and said no more.

32

Just one hour later, Jack and Harrison were walking up the steps to St Mary-in-the-Fields, just in time for the cleansing service.

The church was full. Word had spread that Father Wilson was going to cleanse the church and all its worshippers of the cursed illness that just that evening had killed another and made eight others unwell. Journalists had swelled the numbers, along with a dose of supernatural fans, thinking they were about to witness some kind of exorcism.

Dotted around the church, Harrison could see members of Jack's team. Each of them were watching specific sections of the ceremony and environment, trying to find any evidence of wrongdoing or natural contamination.

Jack and Harrison positioned themselves either side of the nave. Standing up, they could see most of what was going on.

The organ struck up, and the procession began down the aisle, heading towards the altar. All around the church young and old stood up, some struggling to their feet, others jumping up, eager to see what was to happen next.

Harrison lived by the mantra that we look but don't see. It was a lesson he'd learned time and time again in Arizona, and which he applied to every crime scene he visited. He started to systematically look at each and every person in the congregation, assessing their body language, looking for any signs of anxiety or apprehension, indications that they were getting ready for something to happen.

He started with the front row. These were all older faces, given the front row seats out of respect. Closest to the altar so they didn't have to walk far, and nearest to Father Wilson so they could hear and see. He recognised Mrs Ricci, who was all dressed up in her finest dress for the occasion. Most of the front row were ladies, some bent over with age, others standing tall and proud as they gave thanks to their Lord, or gossiped with the person next to them about who had fallen ill.

Then he moved on to the second row, studying every face, looking where their eyes settled and on whom. Pauline was there with her husband. Harrison recognised his jowly profile from the photographs in their living room. Then onto the third, fourth, fifth rows. His eyes grew tired with the concentration, but he was determined to view every single person in the congregation.

The journalists and ghoul fans were at the back. Ready to slip out if they needed to, whether to file a report, or because they were worried it might become too boring or, in the odd case, because they feared the anti-Christ might appear and wreak havoc. Harrison saw the anxiety in the small pale man at the back, constantly touching the crucifix around his neck, shuffling as he stood, and muttering to himself.

He motioned to one of the team, who picked up on him

straightaway. They moved to be closer so they could watch him. Harrison didn't think he posed a threat, and he seriously doubted he was the cause of St Mary's troubles. This man looked to be struggling with his own mental illness; but he decided better safe than sorry.

Other than the man in the back row, there was nobody else in the congregation who looked suspicious or had any unusual body language. Harrison turned his attention to the clergy.

FATHER WILSON SHOULD HAVE BEEN happy to see his church pews filled, but he wasn't impressed that it had turned into a circus. For a man who was serious about his religion, to have his church and beliefs questioned and examined in the national newspapers was not a pleasant experience, and it made him downright angry. He wanted to tell them all to get out. All except his regular flock or those who were devoted to the Catholic faith. There had been one small mercy, though. Neither John nor Stephen had turned up for the service. He'd convinced himself John would come and stir the media circus up some more. He couldn't know that he'd been re-arrested following his antics at the hospital. Instead, he supposed he might be at his wife's bedside.

Father Wilson was a professional. He didn't allow any of these thoughts to cross his features as he processed down the middle aisle. Instead, he smiled piously at his congregation and, once he'd reached the front, he asked them to sing a hymn.

As his church filled with the sound of their voices singing praise to their Lord God almighty, Father Wilson began to relax at last. He allowed their voices to wash over him and rise to the heavens. This was what he lived for. This was his calling, his mission.

As the song ended and the organ notes faded, he took a deep breath in and out, and asked everyone to sit.

'We are gathered today to remember those who we have lost, and to ask for deliverance from the illness which has come to our church. Let us pray.'

He bent his head and listened to the shuffling as the worshippers got themselves into position for prayers.

Then he took a breath and opened his mouth to say the first words of the first prayer, only they never came out. Somebody in the congregation shouted, 'Stop!'

HARRISON WATCHED everybody sit down after the hymn, and then take their cue from Father Wilson to kneel for prayer. He watched as Mrs Ricci reached forward for the bright-yellow kneeling cushion in front of her. Embroidered on to it was a cobalt-blue crucifix. He thought of Anne, who had lovingly made it, and of the huge pile of wool that still sat in her spare bedroom, waiting for someone else to take up her calling. He wondered if any of the other women in their needlepoint group would be well enough to carry on with the task.

It was then that it came to him in one almighty realisation. The needlepoint group. South America. The elderly devotees who fell ill. Pauline's ulcers on her hands. Themba's instruction to *look at the coloured squares*.

He jumped up and shouted 'Stop!', as loudly as he could, booming his command through the church.

There were gasps from the congregation as they all turned to the man who had dared interrupt prayers. He ran down towards the altar, and he could see Jack and the other members of the team following his lead as backup.

Harrison reached the front row and addressed the elderly, horrified faces that looked up at him.

'Please, I need you to stand up now and leave this pew.'

He saw DC David Oaks come up alongside him.

'DC Oaks, get every one of these people a safe distance away from this front pew, then take the name and contact details of them all.'

DC Oaks looked at Harrison in complete shock and surprise, but he immediately responded, shepherding the people out of the front row and asking them to sit on some wooden chairs at the side while he took their details.

Harrison addressed those in the second row next. 'Please, I'd also like you all to vacate your seats.'

Pauline and all the others looked shocked and frightened. Nobody could understand what was happening, but they did as they were told, shuffling along and exiting the pews.

'Harrison, what is it?' Jack asked, looking wildly around for whatever it was that had made Harrison create this chaos.

Harrison turned to him, lowering his voice so as not to cause panic.

'It's anthrax. Get onto the hospital now. Tell them to X-ray Margaret Bellamy's chest, and to test for anthrax.'

'Anthrax? Shit, no! How do you know?'

'Do it, Jack. She needs urgent treatment or she'll die. If you tell them it's suspected anthrax, then they'll know what to look for. Then we need to get hold of anyone else who has said they're not feeling well and get them treatment. Treating it as soon as possible is essential.'

'I sure hope you know what you're doing,' Jack replied and pulled his mobile from his pocket.

'Could somebody please tell me what on earth is going on here?'

Father Wilson walked up to the pair of them, just as Jack turned away on his phone.

'Father Wilson, I believe the wool that has been used to make the kneeling cushions is infected with anthrax. It was sent from South America, where we know that anthrax is still found. The people who have fallen ill are those who made the cushions or your elderly parishioners, who would have sat on the front pews. That was the connection. When they knelt to pray, they would have made the spores on the wool airborne, breathing them in and infecting themselves.

'Those who made them were the ones first exposed. Anne, of course, being the original victim. Anthrax is virtually never found in the UK. Doctors wouldn't be looking for it. They'd see a patient presenting with what looks like flu symptoms, and then pneumonia. And it's not contagious. It doesn't get passed from person to person, only through the infected spores. That's why only some people have fallen ill.'

Father Wilson had visibly paled. He stepped back from the front pew and surveyed his church. The congregation had erupted, with everyone straining to see what was going on.

'I need to send everyone home. Evacuate the church.'

Harrison was impressed to see that, despite his shock, Father Wilson didn't panic, but took control.

He returned to the altar and clapped his hands for attention. 'I'm very sorry, but we have to cancel tonight's service in the interests of health and safety. Could I please ask you all to leave the church building immediately? There is no need to rush, so please be mindful of those amongst us who are elderly or infirm. I will update everyone as soon as we have all the facts.'

The volume level in the church rose higher and everyone started to move towards the back doors.

DC Geoff Richardson and a couple of other officers stepped in to help usher people and ensure it was done without a stampede, and slowly the church began to empty.

Jack ended his phone call and was about to come back over to Harrison when he saw a couple of journalists swimming against the flow of bodies and heading for the front of the church.

'Turn around, please. You've been asked to evacuate for your own safety.'

'Press,' one of them said, flashing an ID card at him as though he'd be impressed. 'Can you tell us what's going on? Why was the service halted, what's been found?'

'I'm afraid I can't tell you anything right now because this is an ongoing investigation. I need you to leave immediately.'

'But the guy at the front, why did he shout stop?'

'If you don't leave immediately, then I will have to ask one of my officers to escort you out, and they won't just take you to the steps. It will be to the nearest police car so that you can be assessed for any impact on your health.'

Jack said the latter sentence with sarcasm in his voice, but they got the message and turned round to leave with a scowl.

THE LAST OF the elderly front pew worshippers were escorted out of the church, and the building became quiet again. Father Wilson sent home the rest of the clergy and was now sitting looking like a man who'd had a shock. DC Oaks, Richardson and the rest of the team were milling around waiting for an update. Jack walked up to Harrison, who was pacing at the front of the church.

'Are you sure about this? Why do you think it's anthrax?'

'It all fits. I'm sure. The missing link was the wool. That was the pattern.'

'Well, it certainly put the cat among the pigeons at the hospital. They jumped on it straight away.'

Harrison looked over at Father Wilson. 'Father Wilson, would you mind if I asked you a question?' Harrison asked and then continued without waiting for his response. 'Anne was cremated, which, in my understanding, is not the normal practice for someone who is a devout Catholic. Why was that?'

'Yes. She was desperate to have her final resting place at St Mary's. She'd given her life to this church. But there is simply no room here for any burials. We discussed it many times, and agreed that in the event of her death she could be cremated and her ashes would be interred within the church, for her to be a part of it for ever. John Bellamy and I are looking for some way that we can do that when the repairs are done to the church wall.'

Harrison nodded, satisfied by the final loose end, and thought sadly that Father Wilson's words, 'She'd given her life to this church,' had literally come to pass.

Jack's mobile rang, and the whole team turned to look at him.

'It's the hospital,' he said and then looked at Father Wilson. This was the moment of truth. He picked up. 'DS Salter. Yes. Right, pleural effusion and mediastinal widening. OK. Absolutely. Thank you.'

He ended the phone call and for a few seconds stared at it before looking up at Harrison again.

'You were spot on. They've just looked at Margaret's chest and apparently it's textbook inhalation anthrax. She's been on antibiotics which have masked it, but not cured it. Now they know what it is, they can hopefully treat her with the right antibiotics. They've alerted Public Health. We're to get out of here now and seal the building until the Health Protection emergency response team take over. Father, they're going to need a full list of your congregation, especially anyone you know who has sat in that front row.'

Father Wilson walked up to Harrison and clasped his hands warmly. 'Our prayers were answered. Our Lord heard us and chose you to light the way to end this scourge on our church.'

Harrison said nothing. There'd been no divine intervention on his part. In fact, it had been a good dose of scientific reasoning and observation, as well as an African faith healer who had insisted he looked at the coloured squares. How Themba could have known that, Harrison couldn't quite explain.

33

Osezua Idahosa wasn't happy about what they'd asked him to do, but he decided it would be better for him if he went along with it. They'd told him it would be included in the considerations when he was sentenced, and the lawyer they'd given him had agreed.

He told them what he needed, and they let him have a couple of his personal belongings back. Now he was ready, and he heard the prison guards bringing them in.

PATIENCE WAS NERVOUS, but they had assured her that the juju priest was going to release the vow she had made and free her from the bondage to Madam. She thought about the big man who had come to her flat and promised her he would make sure the vow was lifted.

Her mind drifted to Florence and her family. They would have been told of her death by now, and Patience thought of Florence's little sister and the postcards she would now never receive. When, if, Patience went back home, she would visit

Florence's family and tell her sister some stories. Good stories, but stories that would warn her never to think about taking the same journey. Not to believe the lies that she and Florence fell for.

The room that the juju priest was in was very different from the last one. This was a small visiting room at the prison, white, functional, and clean. He looked different too, but he started playing the drums with exactly the same beat.

Ba bam ba ba bam, ba bam ba ba bam, ba bam ba ba bam...

His hands beat down on the animal skin drum. Fast. Rhythmic.

Ba bam ba ba bam, ba bam ba ba bam, ba bam ba ba bam...

Sweat began to run down his black skin.

He tipped his face to welcome the spirits and began his prayer.

Beside Patience, the other girls shifted a little, showing their nerves.

Then he stopped the drumming and got up, approaching Patience. He held his palm out flat and blew some white powder into her face. He was showing the spirits whose soul he was asking them to set free.

Tonight would be the first night Patience slept and her dreams would be good.

34

Harrison pulled up outside Robert Mbeki's house and parked his bike. Down the road, he could see Anne's house was still being decontaminated after all the infected wool had been removed. Another elderly worshipper had died in the last twenty-four hours, but now that they were all receiving the right treatment, the prognosis looked a lot better for the others.

Not surprisingly, the story had been all over the newspapers and TV news. DCI Barker had worked hard to keep Harrison out of it after the journalists who'd been at the cleansing ceremony kept insisting on knowing who the big man was that had stopped the service.

He'd barely got off his bike before Robert's housekeeper, Mary, had the front door open. She ushered him through to the sitting room, where he found Robert and Themba.

'My guardian,' Themba said, beaming a huge smile as he entered.

'Good to see you looking so well, Themba,' Harrison replied, 'and, Robert, you're looking better too.'

'Yes. I think the stress of Themba's attack did me no good, but we are over that now and looking forward.'

'I won't take up much of your time. I just wanted to let you know personally that John Bellamy and Stephen Chase have changed their plea and admitted guilt for the attack. It means there won't now need to be a trial and they can just be sentenced. The hospital roof incident will not be good for John, so we can expect a reasonable sentence for him.'

Both men nodded.

Themba looked at Robert, who seemed to take that as a cue.

'Themba wanted to ask you if he could go and speak to John before he leaves for home?'

'Remember, I said to you that the community needed to heal,' Themba said to Harrison. 'I think John might be ready to start healing.'

'That is very generous of you, Themba, after what he put you through, and what he would have done.'

'To be free ourselves, we must respect and enhance the freedom of others. Forgiveness is within us all,' Themba said to him, holding his head high.

'Nelson Mandela was a wise man,' Harrison smiled, recognising his quotes in some of what Themba had said. 'I'll let the team know and they can make the enquiry.'

'Thank you, Dr Lane,' Robert Mbeki said to him now.

'I'd better go. I've got someone waiting for me, but I wish you both well.' Harrison rose from the chair.

'I'll walk with you,' Themba said, following Harrison into the hallway.

'Actually, Themba, I wanted to ask you about what you'd said to me: the coloured squares. What did you mean?'

'It was not what I saw, but what my ancestors told me.

They whispered to me you would be my protector, that I should tell you about the coloured squares.'

'OK, thank you and safe journey home.' Harrison smiled at Themba and turned to leave.

'Dr Lane, I can see the hole inside of you. We must all know our ancestors if we are to understand ourselves. You must keep searching for your answers.'

[LINE BREAK]

Harrison had to admit that the Pig 'n' Whistle looked rather inviting after a long few days. On the way over, he'd been thinking through what Themba had said to him. He was right. Not knowing who his father was, left a part of himself out of reach. There wasn't time to deal with that now, though. He still had the Mannings to contend with.

Harrison took a deep breath and pushed open the pub door. He stepped inside and scanned the faces. Jack was sitting at a table by the window, typing on his phone and with a beer already half drunk.

'Harrison, what's your poison?' he said, standing as he walked up to him.

'Orange juice, please.'

'Really? Can you not join me for one drink to celebrate?'

Harrison shook his head.

'Oh crap, sorry, is there something I should know. Are you like, recovering?'

'No. I'm not an alcoholic. I just choose not to drink.'

Jack studied his face for a moment and then nodded. 'OK, orange juice coming right up. Can't believe I've managed to persuade you to step foot in a pub, so I'll take one victory.' He smiled.

Harrison had a quick check of his emails while he waited for Jack to return. There was one in particular that piqued his interest. The Jersey police in the Channel Islands had a highly unusual case and were asking for his assistance. A dead mermaid had been found on a rock just off a beach and they needed help to work out who the woman was and why she'd been placed there.

'More funny business?' Jack asked as he put the orange juice down in front of Harrison.

'Mermaid in Jersey,' he replied, raising an eyebrow.

'I've seen that. It's gone totally viral all over the world. It's real, well, it's a real woman, not a fake. Amazing job apparently by whoever did that to her. I don't think they've identified her yet. They after your help?'

Harrison nodded.

Jack handed Harrison a copy of the bar menu. 'Looking forward to steak pie and chips, how about you?'

Harrison looked over the food and felt his stomach rumble. 'Sounds good. Make that two.'

'Great, I'll order in a few minutes.'

'Themba Sisulu wants to speak to John Bellamy, by the way. Said he's ready to forgive and wants to try to heal the community rift that John has created.'

'OK. We can put that to his defence team. Actually, while we're on the subject, one thing I wanted to ask you about was Pauline. I don't understand why she didn't get ill.'

'She did. Hers was cutaneous anthrax. Do you remember the blisters on her hands? I think she had Baxter to thank for it not being worse. By keeping the wool in that pot so he couldn't play with it, she prevented the spores from flying around. However, she did get them on her hands. She'd have got ill eventually too, but because her fingers were sore, she didn't do much needlepoint.'

'You have an answer for everything.' Jack beamed at him.

'Not everything,' Harrison replied.

'No. OK, so let's get rid of the elephant in the room. Sorry

I overreacted about the helmet. This whole situation with the Mannings must be one hell of a shock to you, because it's certainly getting to me. I agree with you. That fire is just too much of a coincidence. Question is what we do about it.'

Harrison sighed and gave a half smile to Jack. He'd used 'we', just like Ryan had earlier.

'I need to find Desmond.'

'And what if you get arrested before you can do that?'

Harrison shrugged.

'Look, mate, we need a plan here. My first suggestion is for you to take that job in Jersey. Go and find the mermaid killer and keep your head down while Ryan and I stay here and work out what rock Desmond Manning has dragged his sorry arse under.'

A LETTER FROM THE AUTHOR

Thank you for reading the fourth instalment in the Harrison Lane series. If you want to join other readers in hearing all about my new releases and bonus content:

www.stormpublishing.co/gwyn-bennett

This one took a lot of research, but I always learn a lot while helping Harrison with his investigations. The research can lead down some interesting, but also disturbing, paths. The experience of Patience and Florence is unfortunately a very real one. Young girls and women are regularly trafficked from Nigeria and forced into the sex industry under oath to a juju priest on behalf of the criminals who exploit them.

It is hard to imagine the scale of human trafficking. It's estimated over forty million people are currently trapped in modern-day slavery with around seventy-one percent of those women and girls, and around ten million are children. Sexual exploitation isn't the only reason people become enslaved. Over half of those forty million are forced into domestic work, construction, or agricultural labour, and around half of that total are tied by debt bondage. They could be hidden in view in your community.

Many people hold strong beliefs and sometimes, as Harrison would tell you, those are unfortunately used to harm them.

Gwyn